DON'T TRUST THE CAT

DON'T TRUST THE CAT

KRISTEN TRACY

chronicle books
san francisco

For Max, my little guy, right now and always, always.

Library of Congress Cataloging-in-Publication Data available.

ISBN 978-1-7972-1506-8

Manufactured in China.

Design by Jay Marvel.
Typeset in Adobe Caslon Pro.

10 9 8 7 6 5 4 3 2 1

Chronicle Books LLC
680 Second Street
San Francisco, California 94107

Chronicle Books—we see things differently.
Become part of our community at www.chroniclekids.com.

"You must make your own map."

–Joy Harjo, "A Map to the Next World"

NOTE TO READER:

Nobody believes me when I tell this story but it's absolutely true. One hundred percent of these far-fetched events actually happened to me. Things could have ended a very different way for me. And I'm not alone.

Here are some questions I need to ask.

Do you believe in unbelievable things?
What about lucky stars or the power of moonstones?

If you don't, read this story. It just might change your mind.

CHAPTER 1

The Puke Bucket

What if it's possible to fix your whole life in an instant?

That's why I'm here, in my socks, huddled at the dark end of my middle school hallway, getting ready to practice pony dance moves during lunch with my only three friends in the world: Heni, Rosario, and Kit. To be super honest, which I always am, I've spent most of fifth grade acting like a scaredy-cat, pretending I was cool with whatever my friends did, when really, deep down, I wasn't. I mean, I've got guts. I just don't use them. Until right now . . .

"I have to tell you something," I whisper to Heni. "I have a power dance move."

"Shh," Heni says. "I need to focus."

Without my power dance move, I won't make it. Neither will Heni. As much as we try to understand eight-count beats, we don't. That's why my upcoming move doesn't require fancy counting. I've practiced it umpteen times in my garage. It's fierce. During my last practice session, I accidentally knee-squashed a spider. But that's the thing about power dance moves. The whole reason they're cool is that they're risky. I take a deep breath and imagine my body doing a double kick, cross stomp, swisher arms, shuffle jump. I'm not a trained dancer, so I don't know if my power dance move has an actual name.

"Maybe we should put our shoes back on," I suggest. For all my garage practice, I always wore sneakers. What if my socks don't have the traction I need?

Kit pulls her shiny black hair into a high twisty knot above her head. "No way! Sneaker squeak will ruin everything, Poppy. We need our moves to flow." She dives her hand through the air like a wave.

Kit always says my name like I'm a weed, Poppy, and it hurts my feelings. My parents, Don and Marlena McBean, named me, their only child, after their favorite flower: the alpine poppy. It's not a weed.

"Let's just do it," Heni says, adjusting her headband. "I probably need the most practice anyway."

Rosario shrugs and follows.

If I'm careful, maybe I'll be perfectly fine in my socks. I grab my spot between Heni and Rosario. I actually feel extra sorry for Heni. She has a huge heart but zero coordination. We've been neighbors since birth and I've seen her topple over several times just pulling on her tights. She's just not born to be a performer. If tryouts for our school play make my stomach tighten in knots—which they do—Heni's heart must be pounding like a bird trapped on the wrong side of a window. I give her a reassuring smile. She doesn't seem to notice.

"Found it," Kit says, pressing the play arrow and setting down her phone on the floor. The music sounds so fast as it pulses out of the tiny speaker and makes its way to our ears. I don't bother trying to change her mind again. Instead, I do what my friends do. I dance.

"Five, six, seven, eight. Prance. Two three. And lift. Two three. And graze. Two three. And swish. Two three. And gallop. Two three. And GO FULL PONY!"

At Kit's final command, all four of us work our legs super fast. This is where her choreography gets tricky. My head

5

grows hot as sweat beads form behind my ears, and a small pain creeps through my knee. It's time. As the sound of our stampeding feet softly thunders down the hallway, I pull out my power dance move. Double kick! Cross stomp! Swisher arms! Shuffle jump! I feel myself knock into somebody—hard. Then I hear the slap of a body hitting the ground. Thwack! Heni! She isn't moving.

I rush to scoop Heni up in a hug.

"What happened?" Rosario asks.

Heni opens her eyes and stares up at me in shock. It's alarming to see my favorite friend fully splatted on a dirty hallway floor. "One minute I was going full pony. And the next thing I knew, my own knee hit me in the chin."

"I'm pretty sure it was Poppy's knee," Kit says. "What was *that*?" She swishes her arms at me.

I don't know how to explain anything. I want the hallway to eat me up. Some seventh-grade boys with small bags of cheese puffs walk past and laugh.

"Look who just fell on her butt," Deezil Wolfinger says, licking his orange thumb and giving me a smirk.

I glance away. I try hard never to look at rude people for longer than two seconds so they won't imprint on my brain.

That means hallways at Upper Teton Middle School can be tricky for me.

"Don't listen to Deezil," I whisper into Heni's ear. "You got back up really fast."

Heni stays quiet.

"We need a bunch more practice," Kit says. "We look like losers."

That word sticks to me and makes me feel terrible. Did Kit even see my power dance move?

"Is this actually gonna work?" Rosario asks in a glum voice. Clearly overheated, she slides off her fake leather fringe vest and drapes it over her arm. Rosario wears that fringe vest because she thinks it looks like it costs a bunch of money. I don't feel like I need to wear rich-looking clothes. I tend to wear things that feel soft and have a little shine to them, like wet-look leggings and my lavender glitter hoodie.

Kit punches the air to get our attention. "Just because we suck right now doesn't mean we'll suck tomorrow." She grabs her phone and slips it in her pocket. It has to go back in her locker before class starts or else she risks getting it confiscated by Ms. Gish for the week. She's the only one of us to have a phone, and we all think it's cool.

7

"Why do you sound so mad at us?" Rosario asks, petting her vest's tassels.

"I'm not mad!" Kit yells. "I'm worried. Do you know what happens if we lose the pony parts?!"

We all stare at Kit as she turns a stormy shade of red. I don't like it when Kit asks angry questions. In fact, I rarely answer them.

"For real. Do you know what happens if we lose the pony parts?" Kit folds her arms across her chest and stares powerfully at us.

"Um, other kids get to be ponies?" Rosario answers.

"Right," Kit says. "The cool parts will go to the cool kids and we'll be left to play what's left."

I roll that idea around. It doesn't sound so bad. We'll end up as something whether we practice or not. Why not sit back and enjoy lunch? We could walk the school grounds looking for lost pets. That's what Heni and I did last year. Even though we never found any, we still had a great time. For months, I've seen one cat's photo stapled to every telephone pole in my neighborhood: PRINCESS TOFU. LAST SEEN AT A GAS STATION ESCAPING FROM A SUBARU. Wouldn't we all feel better if we were searching for a misplaced cat instead of stressing out about pony dance moves? Even if we never found Princess Tofu, I'm pretty sure we'd be able to rescue some sidewalk worms.

"Um, maybe getting the leftover parts wouldn't be that bad," I say.

My comment makes Kit's mouth squish into a scowl. "Are you joking? Will you feel that way when Ms. Dance casts you as one of the singing dogs? You know you've got to buy your own costume, right? Do you know how much quality dog collars cost?"

That comment surprises all of us. Dogs? Of course we don't want to dress up like dogs. I own a cat. Heni a fish. Kit a hedgehog. And Rosario doesn't own anything, but often plays a video game where she flies a raven through a wooded area collecting golden eggs. Dogs do seem beneath us.

"Wait. So if we don't make the pony group that means we automatically become dogs?" Heni asks.

Kit nods her head and whips out the cast list. For this year's play, Ms. Dance, the school music teacher, wrote an original musical: *Circus Animal Tricks, Riddles & Songs*. She listed all the parts last week, and Kit has been carrying it around in her bag like she's starving to death and that list is a ham sandwich.

"Do the math," Kit says.

We all look confused. How does Kit expect us to do math with a cast list?

"I don't see the math," I admit.

"We've got two classes of fifth graders, two classes of sixth graders, one class of seventh graders, and one class of eighth graders," Kit says. "More than one hundred students are trying out for these spots. The speaking parts will go to eighth graders. That's a no-brainer."

"How is that math?" Rosario asks.

"This is how casting school plays works. There are two groups where the kids who don't get the major roles will end up. Dancing Show Ponies. Or Singing Dogs."

I scan the cast list. Kit is right. The bigger parts like Troublesome Tiger, Runaway Clown, and Hip-Hop Pachyderm will probably go to the older students, most likely to kids who had serious tap dance, ballet, or Uptown Funk experience. That leaves ponies and dogs.

Kit shakes out her hair and then neatly rebuns it. "I bet you don't even get to sing real songs if you're a dog. I bet you just howl."

I try to imagine how that would feel. To dress in a fur costume and make howling sounds in front of everybody, even my parents. Deep inside my true heart and self, I guess I do feel much more like a show pony.

"I'm trying to save us," Kit says, wildly stabbing her finger at our hearts. "We don't want this class play to be the worst experience of our lives. Our parents will take pictures and videos. Do you want to look stupid on their phones forever? Seriously. Either we pony up or we become dogs."

My mind spins, trying to sort through all the unfairness suddenly being flung at me.

"You're making me feel doomed," Heni says, frowning and blinking much more than her normal amount.

"Well stop *dancing* doomed! Let's agree to come practice at school tomorrow twenty minutes early and pony hard so we don't become losers!"

Are friends supposed to call each other losers? The only time Kit had used this word before was when she talked about Deezil, who clearly *is* a loser, because when he gets

11

bored in his bus line he throws beef jerky so hard at kids' necks that the meat pieces leave a red mark.

"Um," I say, trying to figure out what exactly I want to say. I mean, instead of using the word *suck*, shouldn't we talk about our different skill levels? Rosario and Kit are at one end of things. They're naturally good movers. They stand a real chance of becoming ponies. Since I became friends with them in second grade I've never seen them trip or fall down once. And when it came to gym, unlike Heni and me, Rosario and Kit had never been smacked in the head with a crosscourt volleyball.

On the other end of the spectrum, I know my power dance move holds the ticket for me and for Heni to become ponies. I can feel it in my bones.

But nobody notices that I've said anything. Nobody even looks at me. My cat, Mitten Man, could teach all three of them a thing or two. He curls up on my chest almost every night and lets me talk about my problems. Unlike Rosario and Kit, and even Heni, Mitten Man has awesome listening skills, *and* he's extraordinarily fluffy. Though he never gives me any helpful feedback, because he only speaks *meow*.

12

"Um!" I say again. "I think you need to see this."

All my friends look at me in an annoyed way, which isn't how I like to see their faces. But I don't let it stop me. I unleash my power dance move one last time. I back up so I can bang out my double kick at top speed.

What happens next kind of ruins everything.

I guess I backed up too far, which then made me trip on the puke bucket. *Bang! Swoosh! Thud!* I can't believe I'm on the floor. Now, of course our school doesn't have an actual bucket filled with literal puke in the middle of the hallway. It's just an empty bucket to catch disgusting yellow water that leaks from the ceiling during heavy storms. But before that bucket held weird, gross, leak water, it *had* held actual puke. Isaac Belcher's puke. Everybody knows this because our school only has one bucket and ALPINE PROPANE SALES, INC is printed on the side.

"Poppy McBean hit the puke bucket!" a voice yells. Laughter follows. Lots of laughter.

I open my eyes. A couple people even have their phones out, taking pictures.

Covering my face, I say, "Stop!"

"She got puke water on her socks!"

13

I look down. What a bummer. I do have puke water on my socks.

I stay on the ground waiting for Heni, Kit, or Rosario to come and help me up. There is a huge puddle of water around me and I worry I might slip again without some assistance. Plus, I kind of want them to surround me when I stand up so everyone else can see that this isn't a big deal. That my friends stick with me even when I get puke water on me.

But nobody comes. Like, not even my best and only friends in the whole world. I search the crowd, and there they are: my friendship clump. They're just standing and watching me! Kit whispers something to Rosario. Rosario whispers something to Heni. Heni turns ghost white.

"What happened?" Ms. Gish asks, running up and reaching down to help me. Her bracelets jingle-jangle as I steady myself.

Kids continue to flow around me, giggling.

"I tripped," I say. "I didn't see the bucket." And then I say a thing I meant only to think. "A pony would never do that. A real, true pony would be more alert and aware of its hooves and surroundings and have much better balance."

Ms. Gish looks at me like I've just said something extremely weird. "How hard did you hit your head?" She lowers her round face and stares directly into my pupils. Then the bell rings for class and the crowd of people finally disappears. All of them. Even my friendship clump.

"I'm taking you to see Nurse Vergel de Dios," Ms. Gish says.

I wag my finger and disagree. I didn't hit my head *that* hard. "I'm fine," I say. Which is probably a lie. I mean, if a power dance move only makes my life worse, what else am I wrong about?

CHAPTER 2

Tornado of Fur

I bet far more terrible things happen to all sorts of people in fifth grade and they dust themselves off right away, bounce back, and grow up to become happy surgeons or astronauts or Hollywood stunt people. I'm not built like that. All day long my mind felt sticky, going back to my fall, replaying the faces of my three unhelpful friends and all those hallway laughers.

Now I drag myself off the bus, across our wide country road, gather the mail, and mope toward my front door. Once inside all I want to do is curl up with Mitten Man and maybe eat some string cheese.

"I'm home!" I yell as I turn the front doorknob. But the door doesn't open. It's locked.

I ring the bell. Nothing. This is really, really strange. Mom only works half days, so she's always home, and usually she has peanut butter cracker snacks ready for me. I trudge through the side grass, past the woodpile, and walk around back to the sliding glass door. Inside, it's just our kitchen, empty except for our two dying ferns. I tuck the stack of mail under my arm and knock on the glass. "Hello? Mom? Anybody?"

No answer. At moments like this, I really wish I had a phone.

On any other weekday, I'd head next door to Heni's house. But today is Wednesday, which means that Heni is at the doctor getting her allergy shot. She's still in the buildup phase, which means she gets injected with allergens every week. Hopefully, by the end of her shots, she'll be able to stand next to any plant or tree in the world and also hang out in the same room as a cat. I hope this doesn't sound super mean, but considering how Heni treated me today, it feels very fair to me that she's getting a shot.

Today, though, that leaves me stranded. So I decide to wait all alone in our garage. The deep freezer might still have some popsicles in it. When I open the back door to the garage I'm stunned to see Mitten Man asleep in the corner on a beach towel from three summers ago.

"What did you do?" I ask.

Mitten Man wakes up and yawns, slowly blinking his bright green eyes at me. Most of the time he's a perfectly great cat, but recently he's been having outbursts that are so terrible Mom sticks him in the garage as punishment. I set down the mail, flick on the light, and scoop up Mitten Man in my arms. He immediately begins to purr. By the smell on his breath, I have my answer.

"Did you eat the garlic herb butter again?" I ask. Mom should really remember to put that stuff in the fridge.

Mitten Man gives me a slow cat blink and licks his chops.

"Why would you do that?" I ask. I'm not a rule-breaker, so it disappoints me to see my cat turning into a rebel. I carry him to the freezer and open the door. Popsicles! I grab a cherry one. I hug him to me as I carry him and my Popsicle to the cement steps leading to the inside.

"It's pretty amazing that we're both locked out," I say. "You I can understand. You've been acting like a monster. But I'm a great kid. I don't belong in this garage dungeon."

Mitten Man purrs in my arms.

"I mean," I continue. "Who leaves a friend on the floor like that? When I knocked Heni down today I helped her right back up." I kiss the top of Mitten Man's head. "The worst part is how surprised I felt down there. I didn't *expect* to be abandoned."

Mitten Man rams his head into my fingers, hoping for more attention. I wish I could be more like him. When he wants something, he just demands it.

"And why am I such a terrible dancer?" I say. "And why are Kit and Rosario so good at it? When does all this stuff get decided? It isn't fair."

Mitten Man nuzzles my side.

"The worst part, Mitten Man, is that because I'm not a fluid prancer, I might end up being a dog in the school play."

I finish my Popsicle and lick all the red juice off the stick. "Kit's basically made out of pony swishes and swirls. She'll get a spot for sure." I'm getting upset thinking about how much I want to be a pony. "Sometimes I wish we weren't even friends," I blurt out, and notice some anger in my voice that's not normally there. "She didn't even appreciate my power dance move!"

Mitten Man perks up his ears.

"She's bossy. And sharp. And she whips up dance steps, snaps her fingers in eight-count beats, and just expects me and Heni and Rosario to learn it all in an instant. Which is stupid, because none of us have any eight-count-beat dancing experience!"

Mitten Man unfolds himself from my arms and saunters over to an empty soda box. He threads himself inside it and peers out at me from his cardboard cave.

"I'm eleven. I'm too young to be stressed out," I say. "And where's Mom? Where's Dad? Sure, he's got jury duty. Sure, if he weren't there, he'd be on his propane route. And sure, Mom has her job, investigating . . . all that stuff she investigates. But one of them is supposed to be here, right? They can't expect me to raise myself while all our plants die and the house falls apart?"

Mitten Man pops his head out of the box and meows mightily.

"Okay, you're right. My life isn't *really* falling apart." I unzip my backpack and pull out all my homework. Normally, I wouldn't have that much, but I spent over an hour with Nurse Vergel de Dios and missed a bunch of stuff. I start with the art project because it looks pretty basic. Ms. Gish sent me home with a sheet of black construction paper, a pie tin, and a box of galaxy glitter chalk.

Galaxy glitter chalk is just sidewalk chalk with sparkles.

"Here's some news a cat might not know," I tell him, reading from our handout. "'Idaho Falls is in the path of the solar eclipse. So in eight days the moon will block the sun and everything around us will look dark and spooky.' Wow, that's probably going to really confuse all the wildlife in the area. Poor coyotes. Poor foxes. Poor owls."

Because he's curious about everything, Mitten Man joins me. I place the pie tin on the construction paper. All I need to do is outline the circle with chalk and then smudge it with my finger to make the circle of sunlight that shines around the moon's edge. Heni, Rosario, and Kit and I usually try to make our art projects match. But now I don't know which color they chose. A typical fifth grader will choose white or yellow, I bet. Am I typical? Are they?

I pick up the purple chalk stick and trace the line around the pie tin. Okay, I feel done with homework for now. I look around the garage for something else to do. The mail? I shuffle through what looks like water and electric bills and coupons for a new pancake house.

"Wow," I say. "Something from Aunt Blanche."

She'll be here next week to hike Gnarly Bear for the eclipse, so whatever is inside this padded envelope must be somewhat urgent or she would have just waited to give it to me. Unfortunately, receiving a package from Aunt Blanche doesn't automatically mean you're getting something cool or useful or even nonpoisonous. She lives in California by a zoo and a gas station and sends me random things from her travels around the world, like pot holders, or refrigerator magnets, or foxglove seeds. When I opened the foxglove seed packet, the planting instructions cautioned that the flowers are so deadly just two grams of the leaf can kill a person, which is why Mom made me flush that gift down the toilet. So this could go either way. I hold my breath as I tear through the envelope and bubble padding.

Cool. It's a good gift. A slim white cat collar tumbles into my lap. It's beautiful. It has a small silvery blue crystal heart and a silver moon trinket that jingles when I shake it. I jiggle it over and over to hear the tiny clink and ding.

I show the white collar with its dangling charms to Mitten Man. "Look! It has your name engraved on it." I run my fingers over the metal tag and its tiny sunken letters spelling out MITTEN MAN.

Aunt Blanche has included a note with her gift.

> For Poppy and her cat,
>
> Don't be afraid to dream your deepest dream. May this moonstone guide you and Mitten Man toward perfect harmony.
>
> See you soon!
>
> A million hugs,
> Aunt Blanche

Huh. Basically, I disagree with a lot of this note. First, "a million hugs" would probably suffocate a person. Next, the eclipse is a week away, which isn't exactly "soon." Last, Mitten Man and I already live in complete harmony. As far as I can tell, since the day I brought him home, we've always felt great about each other. I pick up Mitten Man and hold him in my lap.

Sadly, he doesn't enjoy collars or leashes or hats or socks of any kind. He has what Dad calls a "freedom-loving personality," especially in the neck, head, and paw areas. Mitten Man tries to jerk away from me, but I already have my arms around him.

"Even though you're an indoor cat, wearing a collar is a good idea," I explain. "That way if you ever get out and get lost, somebody will bring you back home." In addition to Mitten Man's name, our address and phone number are also engraved on the back.

Mitten Man kicks a back leg loose and smears it across my newly drawn circle of sunlight.

"Don't smear my homework!" I scold. "You're going to wear this collar."

Mitten Man meows ferociously, like he's being run over by seventeen lawn mowers.

"Stop making crazy sounds, Mitten Man. You have an awesome life. Unlike me. Mine is very terrible at the moment. In fact, if anybody should be making sounds like that, it should be me!"

Then, Mitten Man does something he's never done before. As I finally close the clasp, he scratches my arm so hard he draws blood.

"Ouch!" I yell, and it's as if the whole unfair day hits me at once. Kit. Rosario. Heni. Lunch practice. Deezil. The puke bucket. Getting locked out. All this big hurt crashes through my body in waves that I can't stop.

Mitten Man locks eyes with me.

"You sleep all day and eat whenever you want. No Kit. No homework. No bullies. No pony practice. No real problems ever. You just relax and watch birds out the kitchen window. I wish I had your easy life!"

As soon as I say these words, the world goes crazy. The garage starts to spin and a tornado of fur whirls around me. The air turns warm and electric. And how else to say it? Everything near me begins to smell weird. The washing machine and laundry soap. The oil stain where Mom parks the Jeep. Dad's bin of gardening tools and potting soil. My nose detects it all, and the stink overwhelms me.

I stumble and try to go back outside for normal air, but I can't find the doorknob. I try to scream and realize that something is wrong with my mouth. My tongue doesn't even feel like my tongue anymore. It's rough like sandpaper, but it also feels coated in sour butter. Then my toes and fingertips each suffer a deep poke of pain so horrible, it's as if thorns are piercing through them. All at once, every single tooth and bone aches deep inside me and it's like my whole body is getting crushed. Then the bottoms of my feet turn stone cold.

When the tornado of fur finally stops and I'm able to steady myself, for some reason, I'm sitting on the floor of the garage. I'm dizzy and weak and I don't know what's wrong with me.

My hands aren't hands anymore. They've turned into furry paws! I look down. All my clothes are gone and my entire body has grown fur. Plus, I don't just have front paws; I have back paws too. As I stare in disbelief at my back paws, I see something move. It's a tail! My tail! How is it possible that a fifth-grade girl has a tail? When I reach back to touch it, to make sure it's real, I look up and see something so terrifying it makes my ears twitch with fear.

I'm looking up at a massive version of myself. Big Poppy sits on the garage steps, dressed in the clothes I'd just been wearing. Her blue sneakers look enormous, like they belong to a bus-size girl.

Five minutes ago I was fed up with my life and certain it couldn't get any worse. But I was wrong. This is definitely worse. I look up at Big Poppy and meow. If I am a cat, who is she? Big Poppy looks down at me all smiles.

"Isn't this amazing?" she says. "It's exactly what you wanted. You're me and I'm you. Don't you feel fabulous?"

That's when it hits me. I'm not just any cat. I have turned into Mitten Man, and Mitten Man has turned into me. I release a series of panicked meows, trying to somehow get the universe to undo what it has done.

"Shh," Big Poppy says, picking me up in her giant girl arms. "Calm down."

Calm down?! I find it impossible to calm down. I clumsily struggle to break free but I don't feel at all in control of my new claws and fur mitts.

A firm tap hits the top of my head. *Thunk!*

"Be more careful with your claws," Big Poppy says. "That hurt."

Big Poppy holds me tightly as she walks to the freezer and pulls it open. "Ooh. I've never eaten a Popsicle before."

She grabs three cherry pops and tears them open all at once with her teeth, spitting plastic wrapper pieces onto the garage floor, and basically inhales each one in four bites.

"Okay, I'm so done with this garage. Let's grab the spare key. It's so great that I finally get to grab stuff!"

What spare key?

Big Poppy lifts up an empty flowerpot on the tool table near the door and pulls out a gold, shiny key. "Cha-ching!"

She kisses the top of my head and her breath smells like a million chemical cherry blossoms.

Okay, I'm mildly impressed that my cat can unlock my house for me.

"This is amazing," Big Poppy says, carrying me through the kitchen. "Think about it. With my instincts, speed, and social skills, I can fix all your problems."

What? No. No. No. My cat doesn't know how to fix my problems! My cat is a cat! Who should definitely not go to my school or my classes or talk to my friends or anybody else. Big Poppy needs to walk straight to my bedroom and stay there, preferably under the covers, until whatever just happened un-happens.

Before I can think of a way to communicate this to Big Poppy, she sets me down on my bed and I'm overcome by a sudden and unstoppable urge to knead my pillow. *Left. Right. Left. Right. Push. Push. Push.* I can't stop making biscuits!

I am powerless.

I am naked.

And I am very, very afraid.

CHAPTER 3
Death Tiger

"There are rules for being a cat," **Big Poppy says, pacing** across my puffy rainbow throw rug. Back and forth. Back and forth. "Either you learn them right now or you die."

It's shocking the way Big Poppy treats me. Here it is, almost six o'clock, she's just finished eating three croissants and a pint of rocky road ice cream, and she hasn't made any effort to contact my parents. I'm starting to worry that what I'm experiencing is quite possibly a double or even triple disaster. Like when an earthquake hits and you're at the zoo and it floods. Or you fall off the chairlift at a ski resort, break your leg, and discover immediately that all the slopes are occupied by bears. Or you're a cat and both your parents are missing.

"Just remember, worrying about Don and Marlena won't make them get home safer," Big Poppy says, crashing down next to me on the bed. "So don't waste your brain."

Big Poppy is so rude! I got nothing now that I can't talk, so I just stare at her angrily and narrow my eyes.

"I'm not rude," Big Poppy says. "I'm honest. People are funny, they're so indirect when they communicate. Not me. I tell it how it is. Whammo!"

I'm on the verge of making another important observation when I realize: Somehow, Big Poppy can read my mind. How is that possible? Is Big Poppy a wizard or something?

"Relax. If I were a wizard, I would've conjured me some ice-cream toppings and a pepperoni pizza hours ago. It's called telepathy, and it's how cats communicate. Mind to mind."

But Big Poppy isn't a cat. She's a fifth grader.

"Right," Big Poppy says, rolling onto her stomach and staring directly at me. "But you're a cat now, and I'm a former cat, so I can understand you perfectly, but only when I look into your eyes." She reaches out and gently pit-a-pats me between the ears, exactly the way I used to tap Mitten Man.

I close my eyes and try to think an interesting thought to test this power. *Big Poppy has a sloppy chocolate mouth and dribble spots on her shirt.*

"Yeah," Big Poppy says. "I didn't get any of that. Eyes shut, and I've got no idea what's up. So stop it. You should be trying to communicate with me, not the opposite."

That actually makes sense. I uncover my eyes and look directly at Big Poppy. Then I state my deepest wish. "Call Mom. Call Mom. Call Mom."

"Really? Mom?" Big Poppy says. "I actually like Don way more than Marlena. Unrelatedly, sometimes Don feeds me bacon."

I stare at Big Poppy. "Please go call Mom and tell her what happened so she can fix it for us. She's better at solving problems than Dad."

"So I get that you want to reverse this wish ASAP, but before we do anything rash, let's think this through," Big Poppy says.

Instead of grabbing a phone, she opens my sock drawer and pulls out a pair of my fuzzy cozy winter socks that I never actually wear because they make my feet sweat.

"These socks feel great! I always wish you wore these thick ones more," she says, sliding them over her hands. "Ooh. They're so warm."

I watch as she rubs her face so vigorously against the socks that the static electricity makes her hair crackle and lift off her head.

"So, I think we should tell Marlena ...," Big Poppy reaches back into my sock drawer for another pair, "... tomorrow."

What? Why? That's nuts! I think we need some serious help here right away.

"Hear me out," Big Poppy says, kicking off her sneakers and sliding her feet into my Nordic unicorn bootie slippers. "Let's say we don't swap back right away. Let's say we give it a day, and I'll try out for the pony part. I'm a great mover."

Big Poppy shimmies in front of me and then acrobatically springs around the room.

"Think about it. I've got the soul of a ballerina and the heart of a trapeze artist," she says, leaping onto my corner chair and then cartwheeling back to the bed. "I'm all grace and no fear."

I'm honestly surprised by Mitten Man's—I mean, Big Poppy's—flow and flexibility. Until this happened, I guess I mostly focused on my cat's fluff level and cuddliness.

"Don't you want to be a pony?" Big Poppy says, blinking her big, happy eyes at me. "I can make that happen for you."

32

Of course I want to be a pony. And the idea of avoiding all the stress of tryouts does sound appealing. Maybe I'd even be better than Kit!

"Just say okay and it's a done deal," Big Poppy says. "We can call it a night and I'll make us dinner."

Dinner? Did Mitten Man have this ferocious appetite as a cat? Or is it something about being many times bigger that makes you many times hungrier?

"So we agree?" Big Poppy says. "I'll go to school for you tomorrow, snag you a pony part, and then we'll figure out how to swap back."

Okay, think it through. Let my cat go to school for me for a day. What could go wrong? Immediately, I land on a problem.

"What if you go to my school and say crazy things to my friends and maybe other people and damage my friendships and reputation?"

Big Poppy gasps dramatically and covers her mouth. Then she collapses next to me in a stunned heap. "Why would you think I'd do that? I would never do that! We're on the same team, Old Poppy. I want to help you. I can make your life better, don't you see that?"

33

Then Big Poppy bounces back up and proceeds to dance around my room. Her ability to turn and spin and hop and shimmy rivals the moves of professional dancers, at least the ones I've seen on YouTube. Okay, she's right. I'd be stupid to pass up this great opportunity.

"Will you try to be a listener and not a talker?" I ask.

"Better than that. I'll be an absorber. I'll say almost nothing and just *observe* everything that's happening around me. Then I'll come home and tell you all about it. That way you won't miss a thing. It'll be awesome. Seriously. You can trust me."

Big Poppy picks me up and lovingly twirls me around my room. She pauses in front of my picture row where I've hung a series of photos of me with people I really love. Mom, Dad, Aunt Blanche, Heni. And nine of me and Mitten Man, going all the way back to when I was five.

"We're a team," Big Poppy says, kissing me rapid fire all over my face. "And I'll never forget that."

When I hear the garage door grind open, the noise sounds louder than I remember.

"Meow!"

34

I didn't even mean to meow. I guess it's just a reflex now.

"Mom's home!" Big Poppy yells.

She is? I'm so excited! I jump out of Big Poppy's arms and race down the hallway. The carpet feels strange, like the bristles of a toothbrush, beneath my paw pads, and I trot awkwardly until I get to the smooth tiles of the kitchen floor. I swear I can already smell Mom, all brightness and flowers, as I eagerly swish my tail and wait for her by the door. The sound of her footsteps arrives first. *Tap. Click. Tap. Click.* I get to see Mom! As long as I have Mom, it means my life can never be a total pile of ruined garbage. She would never let that happen to me.

The door swings open and she walks through it: dark jeans, teal ankle boots, and a long black tunic sweater. Mom! Mom! I enthusiastically launch myself at her ankles and try to hug her.

"Meow! Meow! Meow!"

"Ack! Mitten Man, you're going to kill me!"

I feel Mom stumble, then reach her warm hand around my belly. I touch her skin with my paw pads as she lifts me upward. I gently curl my claws around her fingers. I swear I

35

can almost taste her honeysuckle body lotion. Finally, after all the day's total rotten terribleness, I am holding Mom's hand. Then I feel a swinging motion, as if I'm being gently tossed.

Suddenly, I'm back in the garage! *Thunk!* On the cold cement floor. I look up just in time to see Mom closing the door on me.

"Your cat needs to stay out there until he calms down," Mom says to Big Poppy, and—

Slam.

I'm in total darkness. Except, I can still see a little bit, better than if I were regular Poppy in the dark garage. I hear Mom talking to Big Poppy inside, but I can't make out all the words. I've heard the word *pepperoni* four times, and there's a bunch of laughing. Just when I'm getting ready to give up all hope and let out a series of meow-screams, the door flies back open.

"I'll come get you as soon as I can, but ankle-attacking Mom is never a good look. Be careful out here and don't pick any fights with garage spiders or that fierce bat."

What? Huh? Excuse me? How is it possible that a fierce bat lives in our garage and I knew nothing about it until now?

36

"Yeah," Big Poppy nods knowingly. "During the night, the garage is a totally different animal. Get it? Oh, and you have a garage thief. If he pops up, hide. Let's see, what am I forgetting? Jeez, I haven't told you about any of the cat rules yet! Do not try to squeeze under the door and go outside—Death Tiger is out there, a dusk dweller and total beast. And the weasels. No way you could survive a dustup with them. And I wouldn't want you to die. If that happens, we probably couldn't switch back."

A garage thief? What's a Death Tiger? Does she mean that mountain lion that lives around here? What is Big Poppy talking about?

"A garage thief is a sticky-fingered criminal taking things from your garage. He's only taken one important thing, which we can talk about later. Death Tiger is a stray tomcat," Big Poppy says. "A monstrous, savage terminator."

"Poppy," Mom calls. "What else besides pepperoni do you want on your pizza?"

"I gotta go. I'll come get you soon. Here's some string cheese."

Big Poppy closes the door and darkness settles over me. I hear a cricket. Then I see an ant. It's moving toward my string cheese! I race and stick my claws into the mozzarella lump and pick it up. It smells delicious. Like it's an entire string cheese factory! *Lick. Snarf. Gobble.* Repeat. Repeat. Repeat.

I consider Big Poppy's warning. What could the garage thief have possibly taken that my parents haven't noticed? And why don't I remember ever seeing a monstrous stray cat? I always notice cats. *Squeak! Scratch! Clck. Clck.* Whoa. What was that? Who's there? I can't see anybody or anything. How could Big Poppy leave me out here? *Squeak! Scratch! Clck. Clck.* Seriously. I'm so scared, my fur won't lie down right. How am I gonna make it all night?

The smell of my string cheese reminds me I'm hungry. While I'm eating I hear a scratch at the back door of the garage. Is it the same sound as before? No. I listen so hard that both my ears turn toward the sound. It stops.

Now things feel too quiet and a little spooky. I move underneath our Jeep and let its still-hot engine warm my back. I hear the same scratching sound, but this time it's coming from the front garage door.

I stop breathing.

Oh my gosh! A paw swipes under the door. Soon a whole big orange face appears underneath the crack. I am so lucky that beast is on the other side. There's no way he can get me.

"Meow! Meow!"

Wait? Is he talking to me? Am I supposed to meow back? I don't want to meow the wrong way. What if I make him angry?

"Meow!"

I stay silent and watch as this fluffy orange and white beast begins to press himself further and further under the door. What I'm seeing is unbelievable. There's no way he can fit. And yet he somehow changes the entire shape of his body and squishes it into the garage. Is this cat a shape-shifter? He doesn't seem to notice me and slinks to the back step, carrying something small, the size of a pine cone, in his mouth. Then I see its tiny pointed snout and limp tail. It's a mouse. A dead mouse! A random cat killed a mouse and hurled himself *and the mouse!* into our garage. Wow. Big Poppy was right! What a monstrous savage.

Now this cat is cracking open his pink mouth and sniffing the air. I hold my breath. He's so close to me I can hear his whiskers sweep across the floor as he sniffs the area where I ate the cheese. What happens next almost shocks the fur right off of me. A hideous growl. I mean, this is a deep, ugly, ferocious grumbling, echoing off the walls of our garage like a clogged garbage disposal.

I want to believe that's just the sound a cat produces after he rudely deposits a dead rodent on your backdoor step. But I make the mistake of glancing at him. His eyes shine yellow as he lowers his head and opens his mouth so I can glimpse his long, sharp, terrible teeth. Fear tumbles through me, and my fur stands up and my claws extend seemingly without my say-so. Wait! I'm a nice kid, with a kind heart. Not to mention I'm armed with zero attack skills. I'm not built to fight a mouse-murdering cat—claws out—underneath a parked car. So instead of handling this like a cat, I close my eyes.

Please go away! Please go away! Please go away!

I'm going to keep my eyes closed and count to three thousand. When I open my eyes I'll see that this has all just been a dream. None of this can be real. I am not, and never have been, a cat. When I wake up I will be fine. Regular. Ordinary. One hundred percent me. Sure, sometimes weird things happen. Sometimes they feel real. But they aren't real. And this has to be one of those times.

One, two, three . . .

If a murderous cat were really in the garage with me, he would've murdered me by now, right?

Four, five, six . . .

My muscles finally start to relax.

Seven, eight, nine . . .

And then I open my eyes.

CHAPTER 4

Shaggy Pants!

Relief gushes through me like a fast-moving river. I'm snuggled underneath my blue cotton star sheets, head atop my doughy pom-pom pillow. It's true. I'm in my bed. I'm normal again.

"Glad you're finally awake. I want you to give my outfit your approval! Too much fur?"

I squint. The light feels so bright. And—oh no. The face hovering over me is so large.

"I've got to go eat breakfast, so come on." She snaps her fingers. "Also, Mom and Dad say we need to have a family meeting, which sounds urgent. I'm guessing either the whole family is moving to a terrible new place or one of them needs a life-saving surgery. Brain rewire. Liver transplant. New butt." Big Poppy needs to slow down. "Anyway, something like that. For real. They've got their serious faces on this morning."

It's Big Poppy, of course. I'm not back. I'm just a cat in my human bed.

"Also." Her face somehow gets even more giddy and hyper. "Mom thinks you killed a field mouse and put it in the garage, so she's probably going to be snippy with you this morning. Which is weird, because you'd think she'd want you to be a mouser. Anyway, I know what happened. Death Tiger crept in and delivered you an expired vermin. Bad first night as a cat for sure. But it will get better, trust me."

I've got too much information landing on top of me at once. I unfold my legs, stand up, and take a big stretch, arching my back until I hear a bone pop.

"How could you leave me in the garage?" I ask her. "That orange cat nearly killed me last night."

It's clear my deepest wish did not come true. I am still a cat. My life remains a complete wreck. But oh no! Oh no! Oh no! I take my first good look at Big Poppy, and my life gets worse. What is she wearing? Big Poppy stands in front

DON'T TRUST THE CAT

of the closet mirror dressed in pants so shaggy it looks like she's trapped in a sheepskin rug.

"MEOW!"

Now I notice her hair parted down the middle, and she's sporting pigtails, which I never wear. Big Poppy looks ridiculous in pigtails. My hair is too short for that style. Instead of curling cutely, my hair pokes out in clumpy spikes. It's almost like Big Poppy wants everybody at my school to know that it's no longer me inside my own body.

"If you don't like it, I can always change," she says. "But before I do that, let's go over your class schedule so I know when I go to lunch and when I switch rooms. Is it English then lunch then Science?"

I pinch my eyes closed because I can't look at her. We shouldn't be planning what she'll do at *my* school. After all the work I've done to make friends and appear normal, the last thing I need is for my cat to destroy my hard-earned life. Why is this happening?

"Poppy," Big Poppy says, plucking me off the bed. "We're in this together. I went and saved you from the garage last night. I stepped over a freshly perished fur pest and climbed under a car for you. So look at me and tell me what's wrong."

"Okay, honestly?" I open my eyes. "You look outrageous. I would never wear those pants. They're the bottom half of a Wookie Halloween costume that gave my legs a terrible rash two years ago. And my hair isn't long enough to be in pigtails. I specifically *avoid* pigtails because they look like *that*." I point my paw at her poky spikes. "It's like you're trying to change me into somebody I'm not. I don't like it."

Big Poppy smiles at me. "Personally, I think change is good. That's why I run away at least once a year. Climbing new trees and discovering interesting stuff excites me." She doesn't seem the slightest bit offended after my insult-fest. "It's how I became short-lived friends with that turtle Raul. Did you know to keep cool in the summer a turtle hides under decaying leaves? Anyway, if you don't like change, I can work with that. Go ahead, tell me what you want me to wear."

Is Big Poppy being genuine? I want to trust my former cat. I really do. But then why would she dig so far back into my closet, choosing things she's never seen me wear to school?

45

Are we really on the same team? I wriggle out of her arms and saunter to my closet, my natural walk now, and lift my paw to a pair of pale yellow wet-look leggings and a dark blue T-shirt with puffy turquoise letters that spell BIG DREAMS.

"Great," Big Poppy says. "And you want your hair down?"

I nod.

"Got it." She tugs out the elastic bands and shakes out her hair. "Now, I think I should take you to the family meeting. But you've got to promise not to act like a weirdo cat."

I release a hiss, which I didn't even mean to do. "Okay, so I got a little excited when I saw Mom yesterday. I feel like that's totally normal considering how awful my day had been."

"I don't want to freak you out, but Mom said that if you keep acting crazy, she'll take you to the vet, and Poppy," she says calmly, reaching for the leggings, "I won't sugarcoat this. That would be too much trauma for you. I'm talking total sensory overload. Do you know how they take a cat's temperature? Also, where are you on your vaccines? You'd probably end up getting a painful shot and the heightened stress would cause your personality to mutate, turning you

46

into somebody you're not. Probably forever. So try to avoid any behavior that would lead to veterinary care. Cool?"

"Poppy!" Dad calls. "Your pancakes are getting cold."

"Dad made you pancakes?" I ask. "Unbelievable."

"Super believable. Don rocks. I've felt that way about him from day one. Let's go!"

With that, I'm yanked up and ferried into the kitchen. Breakfast smells so good, drool slips from both corners of my tiny mouth. Steam rises merrily off Big Poppy's short stack, while a chunk of butter slowly plummets onto her plate. Food has never looked this beautiful. I can't stop drooling as Big Poppy dumps on the syrup and stabs her fork deep into her flapjacks' sweet, gooey heart.

"What does Mitten Man get today?" Dad cheerfully asks, rubbing his knuckles over my small bony head.

"We should give him a pancake," Big Poppy says.

"Reward him for being a total beast?" Mom asks.

Not *total*, I think, but Big Poppy's not looking at me, so there's no one to even receive my joke.

"Well," Big Poppy says, swallowing a giant gulp of milk. "Do cats even have memories? Maybe he thinks we're being mean to him for no reason. He hasn't done anything bad this morning."

Hearing Big Poppy champion me feels good. I release a perfectly pitched, happy "Meow."

"Fine." Mom slides a tiny pancake onto a dish and puts it near my water bowl. "But just one."

I slip off Big Poppy's lap and trot over to check it out. Yum. Yum. Yum. I lick it over and over until the top layer breaks into crumbs.

"Now that we're all fed, let the family meeting begin," Dad says, gently pounding the table with his fork handle.

He's not wearing his robin's-egg-blue propane truck delivery clothes. He's wearing jeans and a pullover sweater, which are his jury duty clothes. I didn't realize the government could make you sit on a jury and miss your job day after day after day, but I guess it can, because that's what Dad did all last week. Based on his current getup, those are also his current plans.

"Poppy, I want to apologize again for yesterday. Getting locked out is serious. It will never happen again. Mom and I will make sure that somebody is always here for you when

48

you get home." He reaches out and tenderly squeezes Big Poppy's hand. "I promise."

Big Poppy presses her lips together and emits a loud trumpet sound. Her squeaks are so loud they make my ears flutter, which I didn't even know they could do.

"You should quit jury duty. It seems like a total drag." She pulls her hand out of his and swaps it for her fork.

Dad winces. "Legally, a person isn't allowed to quit jury duty. You're obligated to sit for the entire trial and then render a verdict."

"Raw deal." Big Poppy pours herself a second glass of milk.

Once I finish my pancake, I jollily weave myself through Dad's and the chair's legs. I like the way it feels to touch him, even if he doesn't realize who I really am.

"What your father is trying to say," Mom says, sounding impatient, "is that with my workload and tying up all those loose ends on the Gilligan case, and his jury duty, we've realized we need extra help with you and the house."

I stop weaving and really focus on what they're saying. In the history of my life we have never "needed extra help." I don't know for sure what it means. Have they hired a live-in

49

babysitter? Is dad's cousin Buck going to come stay with us from Pocatello?

"Really? I mean, it's super tragic all our plants are dying and our house is crazy dusty, but I'm mature enough to watch myself," Big Poppy says. "You don't need to worry about me."

I watch in disbelief as she inhales what I'm pretty sure is her seventh pancake.

"Well, we're responsible parents, so abandoning you to raise yourself won't be our game plan," Mom says, wagging a jam-covered knife at us as she prepares Big Poppy's lunch. "We're not wolves."

"Actually, I watched a show about wolves. They're very involved parents. Pups get raised by the entire pack," Big Poppy corrects. "The narrator stressed that they have extremely dedicated and selfless mothers. Maybe what you mean is, we're not panda bears. Now *those* moms—"

Dad puts his hand over Big Poppy's. "What Mom is trying to say, sweetie, is that Aunt Blanche has agreed to come and help look after you."

"Aunt Blanche?" Disgust rolls off Big Poppy's tongue. "You trust her to be my babysitter?"

Mom tilts her head, which is her go-to move when she's surprised. "You already knew she had a trip planned to see us and hike Gnarly Bear for the eclipse. She's just coming a little earlier."

I guess I did know that, but Big Poppy didn't. Because what normal fifth grader keeps track of her aunt's hiking schedule and also shares that information with her cat?

Dad flashes Big Poppy a reassuring smile. "We thought you'd be happy about it. I'm sure she'll bring a big bag of tricks to entertain you. Maybe she'll read your chakras again. You love her pendulum."

Those words kick my brain into problem-solving mode. Aunt Blanche bought the abracadabra/magic/cursed cat collar. Maybe she will read my chakras and actually recognize the real me stuck in here, then figure out a solution to get us back to our old lives.

Why do I have a feeling it can't possibly be that easy?

"Um," Big Poppy says angrily, pushing her empty plate away, "have we all forgotten about what happened during her last long visit?"

Mom and Dad blink at Big Poppy with genuine surprise. So do I. She's such a maverick.

"Yes," says Dad.

"I know it wasn't perfect," Mom admits.

Big Poppy huffily folds her arms across her chest and glowers at Mom. "Didn't she get arrested? Because of her serious trash addiction?"

Watching Big Poppy fight with my parents at the breakfast table is like sitting through a horror movie. Of course I want to look away from this disturbing scene, but I can't because I need to see what happens next.

"No, no. Officer Masterson merely . . . *questioned* Aunt Blanche about her . . . *contact* with our neighbors' trash cans," Mom says carefully. "And it was a learning experience, because now we know, and our neighbors know, that once a trash can gets moved to the top of the road for pickup, it's considered public property."

"She didn't break any laws, is what your mother is trying to say," Dad adds. "Anybody can take whatever they want out of a public trash can."

Aunt Blanche's trash can shenanigans come racing back to me. My parents seem to be forgetting that she also entered multiple dumpster bins downtown.

"And . . . why was Aunt Blanche going through Heni's trash again?" Big Poppy asks. "I mean, we all agree my aunt shouldn't steal my best friend's trash, right?"

"Not the Kanoas'," Dad corrects. "Our other neighbors. The Stangers'."

"Aunt Blanche is an . . . avid collector of aluminum cans and plastic bottles," Mom says. "It's a good thing. She's a recycler."

With a big groan Big Poppy says, "But it's weird."

I feel like laughing, but she needs to chill out. It's clearly a done deal. Aunt Blanche is in transit.

"Don't tell her that, or we'll end up watching that plodding documentary *Trash Island* again," Dad says. "Remember how much Stravinsky it used to transition scenes?"

With a firm voice Mom says, "It's settled."

And that ends the conversation.

I watch as Mom hurriedly slides an all-jam sandwich into a reusable storage bag and then packs a fistful of baby carrots into a silicone sack. For the first time I try to picture Big Poppy at my school in my cafeteria behaving like a normal human.

53

The scene I imagine makes me go dizzy. I have not given Big Poppy enough instructions on how to be in a public place, let alone how to be me. What if she tries to buy a hot lunch? She doesn't know my student meal number and will hold up the whole line. What if she hears the upper-grade bells and tries to change rooms too early? Will she know that fifth graders don't rotate? And will she also know that she needs to ask for a hall pass if she wants to use the bathroom? I haven't explained how table points work. We're in the final stretch for the pizza party. If Big Poppy tries to answer any bonus geography questions and gets them wrong, we'll lose points and another table could get the party. What was I thinking when I agreed to this? My cat doesn't know how to be a fifth grader.

I need to tell Big Poppy to eat lunch in a bathroom stall alone, then after tryouts she should fake a stomachache and come home. That's the safest route to take.

I'm thinking so hard I walk into the kitchen wall. *Thunk!*

"Do you think Mitten Man's eyesight is going?" Mom asks. "He may need to visit the vet."

54

"He seems fine to me." Big Poppy snatches her lunch bag off the counter. "Sometimes he's a klutz."

I shake my head to clear it.

"Let's hurry, Poppy. If you want to get to school early to practice for the play, we should go now." Dad grabs his bag stuffed with jury duty provisions: magazines, a notebook, pens, granola bars, and Diet Mountain Dew. "Say goodbye to Muffin Man."

Wait. Dad's driving Big Poppy to school? With his propane delivery schedule he never has time to drive me. Big Poppy will get to choose the radio station. Big Poppy will get one of the fun-size candy bars Dad hides in his glove box. Big Poppy will get to talk to Dad all by herself. This feels very unfair.

"And I cleaned the litter box for you last night." Big Poppy bends down and gives me a kiss. "You're welcome."

I try frantically to force her eyes to mine. "You're forgetting your solar eclipse assignment! If you don't turn it in today I lose ten points! You need more instructions!!" But she's looking up at Dad, rattling off a statistic about the death rate of panda bear cubs. Did she get any of that? If she's not looking at me, she probably only hears *meow, meow, meow, meow.*

Big Poppy and Dad race out the front door.

"Why are you so upset?" Mom asks. She pulls a box of kitty kibble out of a low cupboard and shakes it. Hard, fishy pellets rain into my empty bowl.

"It's salmon. Something special, even though you don't deserve it."

It's rough having Mom talk to me with this sharp tone in her voice, like she doesn't even love me. If she only knew it was really her daughter down here, she'd scoop me up in a tight hug and plant a thousand kisses on my face. Then she'd dedicate all her free time to fixing my awful problem. Watching her put on her jacket, gather her files, and ignore me makes me feel fully abandoned. For the first time in my life, it's sort of like I don't even have a mother.

I lower my gloomy head into my food bowl and breathe in the terrible stink of oily fish. I can't eat this. As I stare at the all-yuck kibble, I hear the door slam and the Jeep fire up. Mom's gone too.

And now I'm home alone. Again.

So . . . how exactly does Mitten Man spend his days? Except for the hum of the refrigerator, the house sits perfectly still. It's impossible to feel anything but lonely in all this empty quiet. I need some TV.

I trot into the living room and spot the remote abandoned on the third shelf. Yesterday, I was almost as tall as that. Today, it's unreachable. I hop onto the couch and then take a giant, terrifying leap at the shelves. I made it! But I knocked off three family photos and the silver bell Mom bought in Canada. Oops.

Even with my paws on the remote, I can't get the TV to work. I press Power, but nothing happens. I need more force, I guess, so I push the button again as hard as I can, and the remote skitters off the shelf, sailing into the coffee table, breaking into a bunch of pieces when it crashes to the floor. Both batteries pop out and roll under the couch. Oof. For a lonely cat hoping to watch TV, that's tough to see.

Unfortunately then as I try to calculate a jump path off the shelf, I topple a ceramic plate and that breaks too. Which is truly terrible, because I was with Mom when she bought that plate at the Eastern Idaho State Fair and it has her favorite rooster on it—the Leghorn. I don't think she'll ever be able to replace that thing.

With the carpet below me now scattered with smashed-up junk, I feel something move behind me. I jerk around to see what it is, and glimpse my own swishing tail. Wow. How do I keep forgetting I have that? I carefully leap down and pick my steps, avoiding all the sharpness, and scamper back to the kitchen for my water bowl. *Click. Clack. Click. Clack.*

Crossing the tile floor, Humpty Dumpty rolls through my mind. No matter what anybody did, that egg was a total loss. I can relate. All my life, I've never broken this many things. Overcome by a terrible neck itch, I plop down and use my hind leg to rigorously scratch it. The collar jingles songlike as my sharp claws swipe against it. I don't want these claws. I don't want this furry neck. What happens if my skin and my hands and my fingers and my voice and my real life never ever come back to me?

CHAPTER 5

A Calm So Buzzy and Deep

Everything feels awesome. My hair. My clothes. My face. My elbows. Even the heated air blasting my shoes through the car's floor vents, which I dial to maximum, hits me in an extremely marvelous and gusty way.

"You seem a lot happier than you were at breakfast," Don says as he pulls into the school drop-off lane.

"Yeah. I am. Today's gonna be the best day ever," I say, gobbling up my last Kit Kat wafer from his secret glove box stash. I can't let the news about Aunt Blanche torpedo my first day of school. Do I think she's a terrible person who smells funky and has a lot of hate in her heart? I do. But maybe all aunts are like that. And maybe this visit will be better. To be honest, I wasn't around for her entire last visit, as I fled the home during this time, jumped many fences, and befriended Raul. I smile at Don in a way that shows all my teeth.

"Great attitude and good luck with play tryouts," he says. "Don't work yourself up too much over it. You know what I always say: In life, what's supposed to happen usually does."

A smile spreads across my brand-new dad's face so wide and happy I feel like I could fall inside it. Seriously. This guy's love for me radiates off him like a furnace. It's fantastic!

"Oh, I plan on nailing tryouts big time," I say. "I know exactly what the director wants."

"What's that?" Don asks, chuckling.

"Guts and pizzazz," I say.

As I climb out of the car, he lightly taps the horn, sending me little honks of love while he drives away. Whoops. I should have told him to have a good day. When I was a cat I never had to say nice things to anybody—my life was all about me, which worked really well. But I gotta think more like a human now. Say all those things that don't exactly mean anything, but do kinda mean something.

I stand in front of the school and take it all in. The pine trees. The grass. The flagpole. The bricks. The glass front doors. Other kids run around me like scream-thrilled maniacs. All my life I've wondered what it would be like to have total freedom and five-fingered hands, and now I've got it all.

Good morning, Upper Teton Middle School. Here comes the new and improved Poppy McBean.

Sure, I could honor my word to Old Poppy and do exactly what I'd promised—a.k.a. what she would do. But why would I want to keep her life the exact same? Loaded with problems and worries and terrible friends and zero excitement? The universe doesn't swap you with your cat for no reason. Just like how Old Poppy came and plucked me from the shelter, choosing me over all the other kittens and cats and that one weird, half-molted parakeet. Poppy McBean overlooked my ear mites, eye infection, smoky smell, and partially shaved front leg. Poppy McBean rescued me from that stinky cage and gave me a much better life. Now it's my turn to do the same for her. Does that better, not-stinky life start at play practice with Heni, Rosario, and Kit? No, it does not.

You can't revolt against your old way of living until you learn the lay of the land. Scoping out every detail and smell is important, so I take a perimeter walk around the inside of the entire school building. I look at the classrooms. And kids. And lockers. And squeaking shoes.

Almost immediately, I'm missing my previous nose. Who knew Old Poppy had such feeble nostrils? My old nose could smell every millimeter of this world. My new one has to suck hard to get anything good. Wait. *Sniff. Sniff.* What's that? Mmmm. A yummy odorous sandwich hidden inside a backpack!

A square-faced boy with spiky yellow hair glares at me and asks, "Why are you smelling my backpack?"

Wow. I did not expect these kids to be so sassy. "I'm not, you egomaniac!" I say. "You don't own the air!"

Close call. Reminder to self: Don't let your new nose lead you anywhere stinky. You might end up in the danger zone. I zoom away from that square kid as quick as I can, but not in a way that makes me look hurried, oh, no. I strut away, with full confidence and a mellow head bob. Once I figure out the rules for navigating locker-lined corridors, I'll probably be able to avoid that creep.

I scope out the upstairs hallway twice before I have it memorized. Time for downstairs.

"Poppy!" a voice calls. "Poppy! Wait!"

I do not wait for this person from Poppy's past. It's probably someone who just stressed her out all the time. Not this Poppy, not today!

"Slow down!"

I reach the bottom of the staircase and keep moving, not bothering to see who's stalking me. But my intuition is stronger than even my willpower. I know who's there before she even grabs my backpack and tugs on it.

"Poppy!" Heni says, forcing me to stop. "I need to talk to you."

I glare at Heni like she's a traitorous rat. New Poppy's not messing around.

"I feel so bad. I know I messed up yesterday. I can't stop thinking about it. Please, talk to me." Heni reaches out and gently holds my hand. "I should have helped you get up and I'm sorry."

"*Hi-yah!*" I scream as I karate-chop Heni's hand.

"Ouch!" Heni yelps, like a dog. "That hurt."

"Imagine how I felt yesterday. You karate-chopped my tender heart in front of the whole school. *That* hurt."

63

Then I walk off and start humming "If You're Happy and You Know It."

"Wait!" Heni jumps in front of me. "Come practice pony moves with us. Don't be like this. I feel really bad."

She seems incredibly bummed out and sincere, but that's not my problem. She failed to recognize Old Poppy's specialness. All Old Poppy's friends had a chance to fully appreciate her and they didn't. Now it's my job to punish them. That's fair, right?

"I've actually got something else I need to do," I say. Then I flash her the peace sign and zoom away.

I don't really have anywhere to go, but she doesn't need to know that.

"I just want you to know that I feel bad," Heni calls after me.

I bet Heni practiced that apology a thousand times in front of a mirror. She's good at it. But if you act like a jerk one day, then you pay for it the next. That's my motto. Well, one of them. Old Poppy was such a doormat. Not me. Not now. Not ever again. That's another one.

I know I've arrived at the drama room when I get to a door that says DRAMA. There's a folder hanging on the wall stuffed

64

with cast lists. I read through one and feel stunned by how many cool parts I see. Old Poppy really sold herself short. Troublesome Tiger. Runaway Clown? Hip-Hop Pachyderm! Those sound like much better roles than some prancing pony. With one of those parts I'd really be able to showcase my energy, rhythm, and strength skills in a well-lit environment.

Ring!

The sound of the morning bell so deeply terrifies me that I scream. To my horror, that square-faced kid with spiky yellow hair is walking by me right when that happens.

"You are such a freak," he says. But he doesn't just say it. It's like he's spitting the words at me.

I stop in my tracks. I can't let him get away with this. So I walk right up to him till my sneaker touches his sneaker.

"What's your name, rude kid?" I say.

A small crowd forms around us. My question seems to knock him off-balance. He may be great at hurling insults, but he's not so good at having a heated conversation.

"What's wrong with you?" he asks.

I've always felt that answering a question with a question signals weakness. Which makes me feel both fantastic and slightly tougher.

"Looks like you forgot your name," I say.

He backs up his sneaker so it's no longer touching mine. A clear sign that I'm overpowering him with my energy and brains.

"You know who I am," he says.

"No. I don't." I lean in close and whisper in his ear. "I forget idiots like yesterday's breakfast."

Bam! Sick burn. Score one for Poppy. That kid's square face looks so stunned that his jaw drops open and I can see inside his mouth. I flip around and *smack!* There's Heni. Which makes sense, because I had a feeling earlier that she hadn't finished pursuing me.

"What just happened with you and Deezil?" she asks.

Learning that I just clashed with *Deezil* relieves me. Making a new enemy for Poppy would be a clear violation of my promise to improve her life. But having a hallway spat with a preexisting enemy? That feels totally fine. And since she came out on top, also a huge favor to her.

"It was nothing," I say. "So are you going to wait in the hallway for tryouts? Or what's your plan?"

"What are you talking about?" Heni gawks at me like I'm an alien who just crash-landed on Earth and suggested we steal the principal's car. "We go to class and do our math sheets until we get called to tryouts."

"That's what I meant," I say. I realize it will be a lot easier to tag along with Heni than to scout for my classroom on my own.

I have better instincts than I realize, because my dustup with Deezil was only four doors away from our class. Upon entering, I notice this room does not smell fun.

"You're acting strange today," Heni says, as she approaches a row of hooks where a bunch of backpacks are hanging.

"Blame it on yesterday," I say.

I follow what she does and hang my backpack on a hook. Then I go and find a seat, choosing a desk that looks amazing. Somebody has decorated the top of it with puffy cat stickers that smell like vanilla ice-cream cones.

Sniff. Sniff.

"Why are you at Rosario's desk?" Heni asks. "And why are you smelling it?"

I want to tell her it's because the puffy stickers make it the best desk in the room. But she already thinks I'm acting strange. Maybe I should try to act a little bit more like Old Poppy.

67

"Pit stop," I say. I bounce back up and look around the room, searching for a desk that gives off Old Poppy vibes.

I spot a desk right next to Heni's that looks very basic and clean and approach it slowly, because going to a second wrong desk would definitely look suspicious.

"Are you pretending that your desk might be a mean dog or something?" Heni asks.

That observation impresses me, because that's exactly how I was approaching this desk.

"Yes," I say, plopping myself into my seat.

The rest of the class streams in before the bell, and for a second I worry that I won't be able to recognize Rosario and Kit, but then they enter the room together and the worry melts. They've both been to the house. I know them. Kit charges right over to me.

"Why didn't you come to practice?" Kit asks, her face pink with anger.

I don't have a good answer, so I play it cool and just shrug.

"It's like you've totally given up. Like you don't even want to be a pony." Kit says this last part in a very judgy way.

68

Of course she has it all wrong. I know I should let it go and not correct her, but I'm not built out of forgiving bones. So I politely tell her, "Duh. Of course I don't want to be a pony. Ponies are brats."

Kit reacts as if I've thrown ice water right in her face.

"You didn't feel that way *yesterday*," she spits.

"Listen," I say. "I'm not trying to be rude. But there's no way I'm wasting my talents pretending to be a small, cheeky horse. I have bigger plans for myself in life."

Kit looks so shocked she's shook. Seriously. It's rare to see this level of surprise on a person's face last for this long.

"You have bigger plans?" Kit asks in a snarky way.

"I do," I say.

"What does *cheeky* mean?" Rosario asks. "Are you talking about their butts?"

Ring!

Once again the bell catches me off guard, and once again I scream, which makes Heni scream too. Kit jumps and so does Rosario.

Rosario asks, "Did somebody see a bee or something?"

"Yeah," I say. "But it was just a fly."

Nice for Rosario to give me the bee idea, otherwise I might've looked like a wacko.

The morning unfolds much how I expect. Teacher calls roll. Teacher takes a lunch count. The intercom blasts a bunch of not-super-important announcements about flu shots, play practice, spring portraits, and food donations. I zone out. Rather than listening, I find it much more fun to lightly drum my fingers and dance them across my desk. When you've spent year after year not having hands, suddenly getting ten digits all at once feels better than getting a thousand toys stuffed with catnip. *Dance! Dance! Dance!*

"Since so many of you are trying out for the school play, and our morning will have many interruptions, we'll be completing fraction exercises at your own pace until science time. Okay?" Ms. Gish says, handing out some worksheets.

Nobody questions her. We just take the sheets. I do not know how to add fractions, so obviously this assignment feels very awful.

Here's the thing that's most surprising: I've been at this school for nearly an hour and I can't believe how easy it is to pretend to be a fifth grader. I thought it would take more work. But as long as I sit still and don't say anything, I look like a regular eleven-year-old. When I'm handed a piece of paper I write the name *P-o-p-p-y* on it, and nobody questions whether or not I'm an impostor. Half the kids in this room could be fakesters and nobody would know it. It's all so weird.

"If you get stuck on an equation, feel free to skip ahead," Ms. Gish suggests.

That doesn't feel like a good solution for me, because I'm stuck on all of them. It's hard for me to keep my eyeballs planted on the numbers. I keep looking up and around. Sometimes Ms. Gish catches my eye and shakes her head in a disapproving way, so I try and try again. But fractions seem very stupid to me. So I give my brain a break and let it look anywhere it wants.

That's when I spot something that changes all my life goals in an instant: a desk superior to mine.

I'm not joking. It's a million times better than where I'm sitting. Bright rays of sunshine wash over it, making it sparkle in a magical way. I bet it feels really warm over there.

Ooh. And I can look out the window. Probably my whole life will feel hotter and better if I move to it! Maybe I'll suddenly understand fractions. Maybe ½ of my problem is I'm in the wrong desk. Also, it's totally empty. I must have it.

I turn to Heni. "Who sits there?"

Heni jumps a little at my question because she's really working hard on crunching her numbers.

"Um, Max," she whispers.

"Where is he?" I ask.

"Still sick, I guess." She keeps her head down, working.

I can't believe we're letting the best desk in the classroom go empty. What a terrible injustice. We deserve better.

"Do you think that Max is so sick he'll die?" I ask. Obviously, I don't want that fate for him. But to let this brilliant and perfect desk, covered in light with twinkling sun motes swimming around it, remain empty feels like a terrible crime.

"He had an earache," Heni says, so quietly I almost can't understand her words.

"I want his desk," I say.

Heni shakes her head. "You can't have Max's desk."

But I don't actually believe Heni has the authority to deliver or deny Max's desk to me. I pop up and head to where Ms. Gish is stapling madly at the back table.

"Stop it," Heni whispers after me. "If you move there, we won't be next to each other anymore."

What a terrible thing to say to me. I can't ask Ms. Gish to move two people to one desk. If Heni wants to change how the seating assignment works in this class then that's on her. I'm not here to solve everybody's problems.

I go to Ms. Gish.

"Excuse me," I say in a voice so kind it sounds like it's made out of butterflies.

"Are you stuck on a problem, Poppy?" Ms. Gish asks.

I shake my head. "I want to talk to you about a health thingy."

Ms. Gish stops stapling and gives me her full attention. "What's wrong?"

"I'm not getting enough sunlight," I say. "I think I'm deficient in one of the vitamins. I'm not sure if it's A, B, C, D, E, or G, but I feel tired. My back aches. I just wonder if maybe I could sit in Max's desk. Or maybe move there until I feel better?"

She pinches her lips together and leans back. It's hard for me to read what she's thinking.

"Poppy, remember what we talked about last week?"

Uh-oh. Old Poppy didn't tell me anything about a conversation with Ms. Gish.

"Last week?" I say. "I think my vitamin problems also affect my memory."

Ms. Gish's deep pink lips curve into a smile. "We discussed your chattiness."

Wow. Old Poppy doesn't strike me as somebody known for her chitchat.

"You're having a hard time staying focused today, aren't you?"

I nod.

"I have noticed you chatting a lot with Heni. Do you think you'll work better in Max's desk?"

Ms. Gish aims her gentle brown eyes at me, and her kindness feels so large it surprises me.

"Oh, totally," I say. "You're reading my mind." One lesson I've learned from being a cat in this world: Nice humans tend to be consistently helpful.

"I need some volunteers," she says, looking out at the room. "Madison and Mason, could you please help Poppy switch her desk with Max's?"

Madison and Mason leap into action. Lucky for me, they both appear to have decent-size muscles in their arms and legs. Also, they aren't complainers or grunters. Also, they are extremely good at moving compact things that weigh a lot. As I help rearrange the desks, Kit, Rosario, and Heni stare at me like I've grown a second butt. But I can't care. I want that spot. Yes, originally I wanted the desk already warmed by the sun, but moving my own desk to the sunny spot works too.

"Poppy, I said I was sorry," Heni says, as I slide my desk past her to its bright new spot.

"Everything I do isn't about you," I tell her. Wow, Heni has a very inflated opinion of herself. I can't wait to tell Old Poppy about this. Actually, maybe I'll skip telling her about some of this. Change challenges her, and I don't want to overwhelm her.

Really, what I need to do is get her life in ship-shop shape before I tell her everything I've done. Maybe before I tell her anything.

"Good job, moving crew. Now everybody get back to work," Ms. Gish instructs.

Once I'm at my new desk, nothing improves fraction-wise for me, but that's okay. The sun floods over me and relaxes every bone in my body. I soften into a calm so buzzy and deep that I have to be careful not to let my mouth fall open and tongue slip out. Time for the perfect nap.

The intercom squawks to life.

"All students with last names A through M in Ms. Gish's class, please head to the drama theater."

I stand up, and thankfully so do a bunch of other kids. Cool. I'll just follow them to tryouts. I know I promised Old Poppy that I'd help her become a dancing pony, but why settle for a basic horse if my springy bones and elastic center can deliver her something much more extraordinary? I'm a razzler and a dazzler. I ooze glitz. I can't help that I was born to be a fancy beast.

CHAPTER 6

Clown Out

I'm having my sixteenth daydream about toast. Why? Salmon kibble makes me gag. I angle my belly toward the sun. Until now, I never realized how warm the floor got beside the sliding glass doors. I reach my paw toward a sunbeam. That's when I notice a shadow outside.

The fur on the back of my neck stands up. It's that orange cat again! He puts his terrifying, fluffy face right next to mine and meows. One. Two. Three times. Panic whips through me as his mean glare lands on me like a punch. That's when I realize his meows aren't identical. They have small differences between them. Almost like words. I roll onto my stomach and stand up. Then it hits me: I'm beginning to understand the language of meow! I listen again.

"Meow. Meow. Meow."

"Come. Out. Here."

My fur stiffens, and I didn't even tell it to do that. Having fur is so weird. It's like wearing a coat that has feelings of its own. Inside my chest's tiny bone cage, my heart pumps frantically. I race away into the living room.

"Meow. Meow. Meow."

"You. Owe. Us."

What?!

He's on the other side of the windowsill near the front door. I dash into the kitchen and leap onto the counter where Mom keeps the bread. This feels safe. Ooh. As soon as my eyeballs see snacks, my mouth reacts and ejects my tongue. Gently and methodically, I start licking the counter for crumbs.

"Meow. Meow. Meow."

"Let. Me. In."

I stop my licks. Death Tiger springs out of nowhere and appears on the ledge outside the kitchen window. I hadn't noticed until now that the window is cracked open an inch. Now Death Tiger's slashing through the screen with his knifelike claws and curls a paw around the window frame, using the strength of his whole front leg to slide it open. Luckily, Mom has set a wooden dowel in the window track, so it can't be forced open.

It's as if Death Tiger has declared war on me. What am I supposed to do? And what could I possibly owe him? A fight? He's already shown me what he can do to a mouse. Plus, I don't want to battle anyone with *Death* in his name. I want to be left alone.

I try to be stern. "I'm an indoor cat. Go. Away."

Then I bolt into the living room, leap onto the couch, and bury my head underneath a pillow. I'll wait here for either Aunt Blanche or Big Poppy. If it's Aunt Blanche, she might be able to recognize right away that I am trapped inside a cat body. Ever since her laser eye surgery, she's great at noticing stuff. Then maybe she'll leap into action and get me un-trapped.

And if Big Poppy gets here first, I'll fill her in on the developments with Death Tiger, and she can probably end this terrifying cat clash. Cats probably work out territory deals all the time. That cat needs to understand that this house is my territory and he needs to go be scary somewhere else. Then Big Poppy can get me my peach yogurt and this day's bad luck will be over.

Finally, the school bus cranks to a stop at the top of the driveway. But I don't hear Big Poppy's steps up the front walk. I hear a hundred loud claps and a giant voice that sounds like mine yelling, "I'll teach you a lesson, Death Tiger, if it's the last thing I do!" My hero! But then I get anxious thinking of all those kids watching. I wonder what Heni thinks of all this. We usually get off the bus together, then check what's inside of each other's mailboxes.

I hop into the window and watch Big Poppy run like a maniac chasing after Death Tiger, swinging her backpack over her head like a propeller. Even though she's faster than I expect, she looks really awkward. She waves her arms in exaggerated circles as her legs move in a jerky zigzag pattern. Big Poppy does not look like a natural-born cat chaser. She's not a natural-born human at all, I guess.

The worst part is seeing the squished-up worried look on Heni's face, as she stands alone at her mailbox watching Big Poppy pursue Death Tiger at top speed. Clearly, she feels abandoned *and* thinks Big Poppy has turned into a weirdo. Worry blooms inside me. Big Poppy didn't act like this all day, did she?

Heni walks droopily toward her house. I press my face to the window's glass, hoping to catch another glimpse of her. She always waves at me before she goes inside. Is she going to wave to Big Poppy? I can't see her anymore. Maybe she did wave and I missed it. Yesterday she left me on the ground. Today I'd expect her to be extra nice to make up for that. Historically, that's how our friendship has worked. We fix our spats. Maybe that didn't happen today. Is it possible we're still spatting? Did she go to the mailbox by herself??

I scan the yard for Big Poppy. I can't see her anymore, so I'm shocked when her head appears right next to mine on the other side of the glass.

"I bet you a million goldfish you're in that house all by yourself and that neither Don nor Marlena made it home. Even with your puny sniff factory of a nose, I could smell the desperation in their half-baked plan. Have you figured out how to unlock doors yet?" Big Poppy asks. "Or do I need to let myself in through the garage again?"

Her face looks red and sweaty and her clothes cling to her in a wild and sloppy way. The only time my clothes ever look like that is when I do marathon gardening in ninety-degree heat with Mom and Dad in the summer. And is that a food stain on her collar? Bummer. Big Poppy definitely appears to have had a rough day.

"What are you talking about?" Big Poppy shouts through the glass. "I had a great day. Meet me on your bed. I'll bring you a muffin."

I trot to my bed and wait for Big Poppy. I hope she remembered to turn in my eclipse art. Usually, I make sure my projects get hung next to Heni, Rosario, and Kit's. But since I forgot to tell Big Poppy that, I can't really get mad at her if our art got separated. Mostly, I'm dying to hear about how things went with Heni today. And tryouts. I hope all four of us got the pony parts. If Kit, Rosario, and I got pony parts and Heni didn't, she'll be so bummed out she might not be able to function. Maybe Big Poppy gave her some pointers. Maybe I'm worrying for no reason at all.

Big Poppy swooshes into the room and sets a muffin on a plate near my head. "Banana nut. You're welcome."

The smell overwhelms me, like I'm being clobbered by a whole banana farm. *Nibble. Nibble.* To eat the muffin I have to stick my entire face in it, which feels weird. One wrong move and I could get crumbs stuck in my eyes. *Nom. Nom. Nom.* Worth it.

"I am *so* happy Aunt Blanche isn't here yet." Big Poppy opens my sock drawer and pulls out a thick wool pair. "I don't want to freak you out, but she's a very complicated person. In addition to smelling like frankincense and sandalwood and pickles and having very big underwear, she's got dark secrets."

Big Poppy needs to chill out about Aunt Blanche. "You're so mean," I tell her. "She doesn't smell anything like pickles."

Big Poppy snaps her head around. "Ugh. Sniff her with your new nose and then tell me that. Let's agree not to talk about her until she's standing all stinky right in front of us."

Geez. When did Big Poppy start hating my aunt? "It's possible she might be super helpful," I say. "She's into moon stuff and she's pretty nosy. Maybe she's heard of this sort of thing happening before."

Completely ignoring my positivity, Big Poppy turns her back to me and returns to my sock drawer. I return to my muffin. I've eaten so much of it, and yet it's still the size of my own head.

"You are so lucky to have so many of these." She slides the gray sock duo onto her hands and gently starts rubbing her face. "Also I can't believe your school feeds you as many tuna fish sandwiches as you want. What a great place."

I pull my face out of the muffin. "They don't," I say. "You didn't spend my emergency lunch money, did you?"

All Big Poppy had to do was eat the lunch Mom made for her. How hard is that?

"Relax. Sasha spotted me." Big Poppy rolls onto the floor, crawls onto her hands and knees, and starts doing all these dramatic stretches. Huh. Could I have been doing the splits all along, and I didn't even know it?

"There's no Sasha in my class," I say. "In fact, there's no fifth grader named Sasha."

"Right," Big Poppy says. "I think she's an eighth-grader. She sits with Xander and Frenchie by the back window."

WHAT? "Why did you sit with the eighth-graders? What about Heni and Rosario and Kit?"

Big Poppy collapses as flat as a pancake on the floor. "Those three are super lame. I didn't wanna eat with them."

HUH? Big Poppy promised to go to school and be an *absorber*. She wasn't supposed to say or do anything out of the ordinary. Just get me a pony part and remain silent!

"They're my best friends," I say. "You just abandoned them at lunch? Did you tell them anything about . . . us?" No wonder Heni seemed weird just now.

For the first time all day Big Poppy stops moving for a second. "I actually think they preferred that I didn't eat lunch with them."

"Why would you think that? Did they say that? I've eaten lunch with Heni every day for four years. None of this makes sense."

"Calm down." Big Poppy is acting WAY TOO CHILL! "Lunch went great. Sasha and Xander and Frenchie want to eat with you again tomorrow, and they're each bringing you a cookie."

"What? Why? What are you not telling me? Did something terrible happen at tryouts?" Please let nothing terrible have happened at tryouts. Please.

"How to say it? At tryouts, things went awesome for you." Big Poppy climbs back up onto the bed and exhales dramatically. "And terrible for your friends."

I blink and blink and blink. "More details!" I say, swatting her with my paw.

Big Poppy sticks her tongue out and makes a farting sound. "So, we had to try out in a line of four for the pony parts. And that was a huge problem for them, because there are only three of them. So they added a kid named Pepper to their group."

"Not Pepper!" I say. "She's taken acro dance since pre-school! She does one-handed walkovers after school next to the bus lines for no reason."

"I believe it. Pepper danced a pony jig so spectacular she got a standing ovation. But I think her greatness made your friends' weaknesses really stand out. Even Kit messed up a bunch."

"Wait, why weren't you in their line in the first place?" It makes no sense. We'd planned to try out together.

"Oh, Old Poppy." Big Poppy sighs. "You deserve way better than a small part in a group number."

I put my paws over my ears. "Oh no. Oh no. Oh no." This is too much.

"So *you* tried out for Runaway Clown. Now, they won't post who got the parts until tomorrow, but you did give a *beyond* solid performance, in my humble opinion. Basically, I think it's a lock."

"WHAT?!" I roll onto my back and stare at my faraway ceiling. I'm filled with doom.

"Yeah. I did this runway walk—Hip. Hip. Leg. Leg— then I had to read four lines and run in a zigzag speedy way. And oh yeah, also I screamed, 'Here comes the clown!'"

"Tell me you didn't run like how you were running after Death Tiger on the front lawn, like a cartoon monkey with rubber legs?"

"Oh, great description. That's exactly what I did. And it was a total hit. People practically fell down laughing. I nailed it."

I consider myself an expert at mentally manufacturing worst-case scenarios, and this is worse than any worst-case situation I could have imagined.

"But . . . I don't want to be Runaway Clown," I say weakly. "That's a big part. I'll have to memorize a ton of lines."

Big Poppy points to her head. "It'll be fine. You've got a giant brain."

All this bad news feels unreal, like it's not actually happening to me. I take a deep breath. "So do you think Kit, Rosario, and Heni will make the dancing pony group?"

"Highly unlikely," she scoffs. "I'd say they're destined to be dogs."

I feel so much dread racing around inside of me that I start to see spots and feel dizzy and tip onto my side.

"Calm down," Big Poppy says, lovingly stroking my belly. "They'll make great dogs. Think about the shapes of their mouths. They were *made* to pant."

"Did you at least turn in my eclipse art?" I ask.

"Forgot that. I'll do it tomorrow," Big Poppy says.

"That'll cost me ten points!" I cry.

"I bet I can fix that too," Big Poppy says. "It's super easy for me to make your face look miserable, and Ms. Gish is a total sucker for sympathetic stories."

"Is there anything else I should know?" Not that I really want to know anything more.

"You and Max switched desks," Big Poppy says.

"That's bananas! I bet Heni lost her mind. She doesn't want to sit next to Max. She likes Max." I angle my belly so Big Poppy can reach a spot on my side she hasn't rubbed yet.

"If she likes Max wouldn't she *want* to sit next to him?"

"Oh my gosh, no! She likes him too much for that," I say. "She won't be able to focus and learn anymore."

Thinking about a desk swap makes my mind spin. Ms. Gish only reassigns desks when something goes wrong. "Did something happen in class to make her switch the desks around? Did anybody else get switched?"

Big Poppy looks at me slowly. "If I tell you the truth, will you promise not to freak out?"

"Maybe?" I'm not sure I've got enough energy to freak out.

"I asked Ms. Gish to give me Max's desk."

Wow. Big Poppy is the worst absorber that has ever lived. "Why would you do that? Does Heni know this? She will hate me if she knows I made it happen on purpose." I am shocked. My cat went to school for me and basically wrecked my whole life *and* all the lives of my friends in *one* day. I had no idea I owned an animal filled with so many destructive impulses.

"Well," Big Poppy says, way too calmly, "I didn't know Heni had weird feelings for Max. But what can I say? I went to school and did my best. Was Heni freaked out that I wanted to switch desks? Yes. Did she plead with me to stop? Totally. Did I? Of course not. Max had the sunny desk."

I feel my heart beating a million thumps a minute. "You said we were on the same team, but you're acting like a wrecking ball!"

"It's a bummer you feel that way."

A bummer. That's all she's got to say for herself? "Okay. We need to end this right now. The switch didn't work out. Game over. It's time for me to fix everything. We need to switch back."

"That's so rude, Old Poppy! I don't deserve all these insults." She sounds genuinely offended. "It was my first day as a fifth grader. There's a ton of things I had to learn in an instant."

"I get it," I tell her. "You weren't built to be an eleven-year-old. And I'm not built to be a cat. It's fine. We just need to fix it now."

"Whoa, I think I'm much better at being you than you are at being me. Like I said, *I* had a great day. *You* knocked

90

a trillion things off the shelves in the living room and broke the remote."

I can't believe how snobby and selfish Big Poppy sounds. I must get out of this cat body immediately. "We both need to wish what we wished before," I say.

"You're so bossy. Can I have a slice of pizza first?"

"No!" I say. "I'll give you a whole pizza after we switch back. It'll be the size of a motorcycle. You'll love it."

"You're being mean to me right now. I worked powerfully hard to improve your life today!"

"All I wanted you to do was get me a pony part and now I'm a giant clown!"

"A regular-size clown!"

As my anger toward Big Poppy balloons inside me, I feel my ears flatten against my head. "I want my life back!" I shout.

"Fine!" Big Poppy spits back at me. "Take your terrible life back."

I gasp. What an awful thing to say to me. My life is not terrible. Sure, I struggle a little. I let what others think about me change how I feel about myself. And sometimes, I feel lonely and misunderstood even when I'm with my friends.

DON'T TRUST THE CAT

But that's not *terrible*. That's only slightly bad. And a slightly bad life is way better than being a fur-covered animal without thumbs or parents! Really, other than my friends possibly getting stuck as singing dogs for the school play, and losing a few points on my art project, all the stuff Big Poppy messed up is still fixable. Nothing is trashed forever. *Breathe. Breathe.* Slightly bad or not, my life is mine.

I close my eyes and make my exact wish again. "You sleep all day and eat whenever you want. No Kit. No homework. No bullies. No pony practice. No real problems ever. You just relax and watch birds out the kitchen window. I wish I had your easy life!"

Nothing happens.

"You did it wrong," Big Poppy says. "You just wished to be a cat again. You need to wish the opposite. *I* need to say the words you just said. Duh."

What? Oh, right. "Okay. This is all very stressful. You're right. You say those words for your wish. What do I say for mine?"

I suddenly realize that I don't know what Mitten Man was thinking when the swap happened.

"You're asking for the exact words?" Big Poppy asks. "From yesterday? From my cat brain?"

"Yes!" I say. I feel like Big Poppy enjoys dragging out this process.

"Hmmm," Big Poppy hums while tapping her head.

I try not to freak out and instead pretend to be patient.

"Oh, I remember. I thought, 'I wish Poppy felt happy.'"

Ouch. That stings a little. Big Poppy's thought actually seems super considerate, and I wasn't expecting that.

"Are you sure that's what you were thinking?" I ask. At the moment it's hard to trust my former cat one hundred percent.

Big Poppy nods her head. "You hold me too tight when you're sad."

I didn't realize that my cat understood what was happening inside me based on how I held him. I guess he's been a better listener than I recognized. I close my eyes and focus and say my wish.

"I wish Poppy felt happy. Also, I want to be Poppy Mc-Bean again. I want my old life back. Right now. Please." I wait for the fur tornado. The energy spin. The change.

Nothing.

I open my eyes. "Did you do it?" I ask.

"Yes," Big Poppy says.

Should I believe her? "We need to do it again and this time you need to say it out loud," I firmly instruct.

"When you yell at me it makes me *not* want to cooperate," Big Poppy says.

"Aurggg!" I scream.

"Okay. Calm down. Fine," Big Poppy says. "I'll do it."

I listen as the wish falls out of Big Poppy's mouth. At the same time I release my wish in my mind.

Zilch. Nada. I remain a cat.

"Maybe we need to do it in the garage?" Big Poppy suggests.

She's right. We need to release the wish in the exact same place. How could I overlook such an important part of un-cursing a curse? "Let's go!"

Big Poppy opens the door and I climb onto the cement step. The cold surface chills the bottoms of my tiny paw pads.

Without wasting time, Big Poppy says the wish out loud. I say my wish in my head using the exact words: *I wish*

Poppy felt happy. I fully expect the magical swap to happen. But we wait. And wait. And wait.

"When do I get my pizza?" Big Poppy asks.

"Why isn't this working?" Big Poppy should be just as stressed out and anxious as I am. How can she be so calm?

"Maybe you're right, and rotten as she is, Aunt Blanche will redeem herself by knowing what to do," Big Poppy says. "No reason to waste one more minute of our lives going berserk in this garage."

I want to try again. I don't want to admit that I'm stuck inside my cat's body with no real plan to get out.

Big Poppy gently pets my head. "Maybe I can fix the remote and find something for you to watch on TV. Maybe a documentary! There's a great one about Genghis Khan. Did you know he taught his cheetahs to fetch?"

I've never heard of Genghis Khan. And I don't want to learn about him, even though I do think it's cool a cheetah can be taught to fetch. I feel tears forming in my small cat eyes.

"I just . . ." I wish cats could cry, but that doesn't seem to be working. "Things are going really, really, extremely terrible right now."

Big Poppy reaches for the doorknob. "All journeys have a few bumps."

"*Bumps?*" Um, I think these are a little more than *bumps*! "My most important friendships have been turned upside down, I poop in a box, I'm a clown, I'm losing points on my art, my desk got moved, I'm covered in fur, my mom basically hates me, plus she feeds me fish pellets, and a very mean cat has started yelling at me through the windows," I sob. "I mean, I think he wants to break into the house and fight me."

Big Poppy lets go of the doorknob and turns back around. "Jeez, don't melt down." Even though her words aren't very sympathetic, her face is. "I'll do better tomorrow with your friendship glob. And don't worry about Death Tiger. There's no way he's getting inside unless you take out the dowel and let him in. You're perfectly safe. And I promise to always clean out your litter box. Every day that we're stuck like this."

A single tear tumbles out of me before I say anything. "I want my friends to still be there for me when I go back to school." A second tear rolls down my nose and plops onto the garage floor, splattering into a sad, wet blob.

Big Poppy picks me up. "I said I'll do better," she says, gently stroking my head. "Really, I mean it."

Sniffle Sniffle. "Can you write Heni a note and apologize?" I ask.

"Huh?" Big Poppy says. "Why?"

"That's what friends do," I say.

Big Poppy blinks at me and then shrugs. "Sure. Just tell me what to say."

My problems don't feel quite solved, but at least I can try to patch things up with Heni. Big Poppy pauses in the kitchen to tilt a family-size bag of mini mustard pretzels to her mouth. Like a magician, she makes the bag's contents entirely disappear. Then she carries me into our bedroom and grabs a pen and a piece of pink paper from the desk.

"Okay," she says. "What do you want to tell Heni?"

My ears perk up into perfect triangles. "Maybe I should explain that I'm a cat!" We've been friends for so long, she must suspect something is seriously wrong with me. "If I told her the truth about the switcheroo, she'd be super understanding and she wouldn't be mad at me at all."

Big Poppy's eyes grow big, like two stunned moons. "Um, that's a completely cuckoo idea. I think you're so sad you actually broke your brain. There's no way anyone would believe that." My own brown eyes are full of pity.

97

"But what if Heni does?" I ask.

Big Poppy sets down the pen and aims my own eyes at me again. "What if she doesn't? You'll seem so weird that you'll probably lose her as a friend."

Lightning strikes my heart. I try to swallow, but tears burn so hot behind my eyeballs that my throat tightens. Could that be true?

Thinking of *not* telling Heni the truth, after thinking I would, makes the last bits of happiness shrivel inside me.

"Wow," Big Poppy says. "I didn't realize that news would crush you. Fine. We can tell her. I was born a gambler anyway."

I bury my head in my paws. "I don't want to lose Heni."

"I'll try to keep that from happening. Why don't we start your letter to Heni like this:

Dear Heni,

I am writing you a note.

Who among us doesn't have a few funky flaws? And we'll need to draw a GIANT sad face here."

"Wait. Are you sure that doesn't sound weird?" I ask.

"No way. It's a perfect start," Big Poppy gushes.

So we keep writing.

> Dear Heni,
>
> I am writing you a note.
>
> Who among us doesn't have a few funky flaws?

> Today my flaws were not my fault. What I am
> about to say is unbelievable, but trust me THIS is
> the TRUTH. I am currently a CAT. You might think
> that's impossible. It's not. It happened very easily. I
> am now Mitten Man and Mitten Man is now me. I'm
> trying to fix this and I might need your help. Maybe
> you've heard of this happening before? I need you to
> believe me. To prove to you this is all true, when you

next see me (I look like Mitten Man) I will wink at you. As you know, it's actually very hard for me to wink, so that's how you will know it's me. I miss you so much. Being a cat is very hard. Eating cat food makes me sad. I hope you will forgive me.

Who/What do you forgive?

☐ Poppy McBean

☐ Bats

☐ Cats

☐ Wombats

Who/What do I forgive?

☒ Heni Kanoa (forgiven days ago)

☒ Power dance moves

☒ Ponies

☒ Puke buckets

CHAPTER 7
Alarm Me

The thought of giving Heni this note really bugs me. What if it makes her head explode? Or worse, what if it leads to a weird conversation about her feelings? Clearly, I can't tell Heni that her best friend is a cat. I've got a real problem on my hands. Seriously. How many promises is a fifth grader expected to keep? ½? ¼? Three out of a gazillion?

"So I heard from Aunt Blanche, and even with Mercury in retrograde, she 'estimates' she'll arrive tonight," Marlena says, rolling her eyes and wringing a second lemon slice into her steaming tea.

"So she gets a total pass on her last visit?" I ask.

"Yes," Don and Marlena say in unison.

I feel like I could vomit, but I swallow hard instead.

Trying to get my attention, Old Poppy starts meowing at the highest decibel level a cat can generate sound.

"What is *wrong* with that cat?"

Marlena is nearing the edge, I can feel it. Poppy's parents fret like a naked mole rat digs. Fearing Marlena might suggest—again—that we take Old Poppy to the vet, I decide to be brutally honest. "I think that cat hates Aunt Blanche."

"Poppy, don't say that," she replies. "Aunt Blanche is a good, good woman, and if Mitten Man knew anything, he'd know that."

Don rolls his eyes. Even he's not buying it. "She's perfectly okay," he says.

"Let's think about this," I say. "Dad's jury duty will end soon. Your Gilligan case won't last forever, right? I'm fine just coming home and doing my homework and eating toast. Let's stick to the old plan and tell her to come next week and hike Gnarly Bear."

"NO!" Poppy's parents say in unison.

"All day long I deal with cheats and liars. I track them. I photograph them. Working for the insurance company, I see things the average person never does." Marlena's in intense mode. "There are bad people in this world, Poppy McBean. Criminals lurk in every neighborhood."

102

Don lovingly pats my hand and says, "Let's not traumatize our child." Man, Don is the absolute best. "What Mom means is that it's good to have an adult around in case something goes wrong."

"Cool," I say. But things are far, far from cool. It's starting to dawn on me the actual dangers involved with this visit. Not for me, but for Old Poppy. In addition to smelling a little bit like the spice rack *and* pickles, Aunt Blanche has a thing against *indoor* animals. I haven't told anybody this, but the reason I ran off and made friends with Raul last time was because Aunt Blanche cornered me one night and said, "Your soul was meant to be wild. It's time for you to go make your mark on this world!" Then she tossed me outside and shut and locked the door.

She meant well. Sure. But anyone who's not a Fresno hippie knows that you don't put a cat outside at night in rural Idaho. Darkness is a death trap for a well-mannered house cat. Twilight-dwelling animals slink through backyards and fields hoping to devour a hot meal. A hawk, skunk, raccoon, fox, weasel, or coyote would happily polish off any cat. Indoor cats are called *indoor cats* for a reason. We're not craving to eat our meals alfresco. We're interested in laser dots and catnip. Aunt Blanche can keep her cougar-populated wonderland all to herself.

I'll have to keep a sharp eye out for Old Poppy. She's not scrappy enough to endure something like that.

"Ready to head out?" Don asks.

"I sure am," I say. Love riding to school with Don!

Plus, avoiding the bus seems smart. The last thing I want to do is hand Heni this schmaltzy note aboard a moving vehicle. I'd be trapped. As soon as she reads it she's going to want to talk about it. The smarter plan would be to leave it in her desk. Maybe I can hide it under something and it'll take her weeks or maybe months to find it.

This all feels so complicated. Is it my fault that self-sacrificing relationships with fifth graders don't come naturally to me?

Marlena kisses me goodbye and hands me a lunch bag. "Go have the best day ever!"

"*Tu-whit tu-whoo!*" I whistle-sing.

Don and Marlena glance at each other.

"What did you say?" Marlena asks me.

I shrug. "*Tu-whit tu-whoo*. It's the celebratory cry of the tawny owl." Should I be trying harder to sound like Old Poppy? Or should I be enjoying what I have while I have it? It feels like I should know the answer to this question, but I don't.

"I never knew you mimicked owls," Don says.

"Just the ones that sound cool," I tell him.

"Your cat is following you," Don informs me as we make our way to the front door.

Oops. I forgot to make Old Poppy toast. I scoop her up off the floor. "Opening the bread box is easy," I whisper in her ear. "Attack the pumpkin loaf after we leave. I'll clean up any counter crumbs when I get home. You're welcome."

I can tell she's seriously upset with me for ignoring her throughout breakfast, because she claws my hand as I gently toss her onto the couch.

"Goodbye!" I call behind me. "Don't do anything I wouldn't do."

Should I have taken the time to properly warn Old Poppy about Aunt Blanche's foolish hippie theories? Probably.

Should I have disclosed the location of my three favorite hiding spots unreachable by human arms? Yeah. But Old Poppy will understand that on school days my schedule runs tight. I'll fill her in when I get home. Aunt Blanche won't be here till tonight anyway.

Out of all the perks of being a real-life fifth grader, riding in a car and eating mini candy bars with a dude who loves me unconditionally is the best. Poppy really won the dad lottery. Part of the joyful ride comes from watching the scenery fly past me and looking for birds. My new eyes aren't as sharp as my old ones, but where I look hard enough, I can see them everywhere: atop telephone poles, tucked in trees, perched on fence posts, soaring under fluffy clouds.

"What are you looking at out there?" Don asks.

"Robin. Starling. Bluebird."

Don flips up his visor and squints into the sky. "Good eyes."

"They could be better," I say regretfully.

"You've got twenty-twenty vision. It actually doesn't get better than that," he compliments.

I smile at Don. It's so sweet how he appreciates even the amazingly basic stuff about me.

"Hey, kiddo, your owl factoid reminded me we haven't played pop quiz geography in a long time. Before I drop you off, let's go. Hit me with some Gem State trivia."

What? Is this a joke? Why would I want to play trivia? We were having a great time looking for birds.

"I'll go first. What's the tallest mountain in Idaho?"

"Um," I say. Big yikes. I didn't realize Old Poppy was an expert in mountain elevation. "That's a tough one."

"You're right." He pauses and I die a little more. "I'll help you. Mount Borah. It's in the Lost River Range in Salmon-Challis National Forest. Remember? That's the one I tried to climb once with my friend Bernie, but neither of us brought an ice axe, so we never made it past Chicken Out Ridge?"

I feel panicked. I can tell he wants to lob another question at me. And he does!

"So, have you noticed my sweater yet?" he asks.

What's gotten into Don? Yesterday Don was way, way more chill. I glance at Don's sweater. "It's green."

"It's my birthday present," he says. "From last year."

Why is Don talking about his birthday presents? I don't care about birthday presents.

107

"You gave it to me," he says. "Usually you comment when I wear your gifts."

Uh-oh. I'm suddenly on shaky ground. Does Don want a compliment? Or something deeper?

"I love that sweater," I say. "It makes you look like a kiwi. All fuzzy and green."

His face looks alarmed. "It does?"

Double uh-oh. Maybe comparing a person to a kiwi isn't a compliment. Luckily just then we pull into the drop-off lane at school. But instead of unlocking the doors, Don reaches out and pats my knee.

"Hold on. You know what I'm really thinking about?" he asks. "*Your* birthday."

"Why?" I ask. As a cat, I don't think anybody ever recognized my birthday.

"I want to talk to Mom and see if we can get you a phone," he says, eyes beaming with a happiness rarely seen in this lifetime. "What do you think?"

I consider it. Maybe I do care about birthday presents. But does Old Poppy really need a phone? "What about something more useful?"

His smile crashes. "But last week you said it was the only thing you wanted."

"A lot can change in a week. What about getting me something the whole family could enjoy?"

"Like what?" he asks.

"A carpeted wooden cat tower, four levels, with perches and a tunnel, and a built-in sisal rope scratch post?" I move my hands toward the truck's ceiling so he can see I mean for it to be dramatically tall.

"Poppy, the gift should be for you. Plus, how would the whole family be able to enjoy a cat tower?"

I open my eyes wide and blink them a bunch so I appear very sincere. "Dad, nothing makes me happier than watching Mitten Man play. And aren't you and Mom happiest when I'm happy?"

"Geez. My kid's got a heart of gold. I offer her a phone and she wants a toy for her cat."

"Not a toy. A four-story cat tower," I correct.

Outside my window, students tramp across the grass to get to the building. I can't believe I'm still here. I've got places to be and people to avoid.

109

"Great talk," I say. "But I don't want to be late for school."

"Hey, when Aunt Blanche gets here tonight, try to be extra sweet to her. She really is doing us a huge favor by coming early."

"I'll try," I say. My voice sounds so chipper it's almost like I'm singing, which surprises me because my life isn't nearly as awesome as it was yesterday. It's turned a little bit soupy with talkative Don, friendship drama, and my growing distrust in a bad-news aunt.

"Love you!" he calls to me as I slam the door.

"Ditto!" I reply.

I bolt from the car and run at a speed that most people probably use when being ambushed by a moose. Spoiler alert: I'm great at sensing an ambush. And the closer I get to the school, the more certain I become that Poppy's desperate friends are planning to confront me. If I can make it to the classroom and drop off this note, and then hurry to the bathroom and lock the door and hide, I'll be totally safe. Then I can go to class, pretend to learn, find out I'm a clown, smile at the friendship glob, agree with the friendship glob, hide in bathroom again if this shaky plan falls apart, ride the bus home, and tell Poppy I did everything the way she wanted it done. Crisis avoided, I hope. As I zoom into the school, I consider maybe hiding out in the boys' bathroom for extra protection. I really doubt anybody would go looking for Poppy McBean in there.

Regrettably, before I make it to the bathrooms, Heni spots me.

"Poppy! Wait!" Heni calls.

I pivot and speed up my run. I doubt she can catch me. After pounding two fun-size Kit Kats, I'm on a full-blown sugar high.

Smash!

I can't believe my terrible luck. How did I end up on the floor again? I look up and see a person I really didn't want to clap eyes on ever again: Deezil Wolfinger. I can't tell if he tripped me on purpose or if he has big feet. Maybe both.

"Dork down," Deezil crows, like the bully he is.

He actually seems surprised that I'm pasted to the floor, so I don't think he intended to hallway-clobber me. It just happened.

"Let me help you up," Heni says. She zips to my side at light speed and thrusts her arm out so fast it blurs.

Ugh. *I GET IT, HENI.* This doesn't make up for the puke bucket! Bleh. Heni's face looks as bright as a Christmas tree. I accept her hand, even though I want to create distance between us. While I'm getting up I notice a giant, smashed spider on the side of Deezil's shoe.

"Yuck," I say. I mean, it's the biggest spider I've ever seen in my life. And I've spent a ton of time on the ground, sniffing out cobweb corners.

"Yuck to you too," Deezil spits back.

"Triple yuck to your squashed shoe spider! That thing is a beast!"

Deezil smiles at me in a wicked way. "So you're afraid of a hobo spider, huh?"

Then he wiggles his shoe near my face and those spider's spindly dead legs twitch a little and I react super fast. I powerfully kick his shoe away with my right sneaker. Twice.

"Hi-yah!" I yell.

Everybody in the hallway is super surprised when Deezil's shoe flies off and he goes down on his butt, even me. I can feel Heni breathing on me in a nervous way. It's such a bummer she's decided to glue herself to me today of all days.

So I turn to run the other way. Terrible news. Kit and Rosario are storming toward me. I'm fully trapped. My eyes dart around looking for an escape path. There's none.

"We're not finished, dork," Deezil says from the ground.

"What's going on?" Rosario demands.

"Did you just ankle-tackle Deezil Wolfinger?" Kit spits at me.

Ugh. Why is middle school such a zoo? I full-on ignore their questions and run-walk to Ms. Gish's class, the whole friendship blob chasing after me.

I make it to my desk, throw my head down on my arms, and close my eyes. Maybe if I sit perfectly still, they'll leave me alone.

Snap. Snap. Snap.

I open my eyes and see Kit's fingers rudely snapping near my nose. They smell like donuts. I squeeze my eyes shut again.

"We need to talk," Kit says. "We're not cool with any of this. Especially yesterday!"

I hear my class trickling into the classroom, while somebody, probably Ms. Gish, squeakily polishes the white board.

"Okay," I say. "Let's talk about it over lunch."

"No," Kit says. "Open your eyes. We want to talk about it right now."

Drat. I open my eyes.

"What's your deal?" Kit asks, stabbing her finger at me.

I can't believe Old Poppy remains friends with such a bossy finger-stabber. If my choices were these three or nothing, I would eat by myself in a back corner every day.

"Stop acting like you can't hear me and answer my question," Kit demands, flipping her dark hair over her shoulder. "What's your deal? First, you unleash a power move that knocks half of us down. Then, out of nowhere, you force a desk swap. Next, you ditch us and stick us with Pepper, a star so bright anybody standing next to her looks lousy— and then desert us at lunch for eighth graders."

Her anger lands on me like a bomb. I try to defuse it with a giant smile and a shrug. "What's so wrong with liking power dance moves, wanting to be a clown, and expanding my social circle?" I ask. I really do not want to be talking

114

to them. But I feel obligated not to explode. I have to make sure they stay friends with Old Poppy. This is impossible.

"Why didn't you tell us you wanted to be a clown?" Heni asks.

Her lips pinch together in a worried way. Of the blob, she's the one who seems to truly be suffering. I look away.

"Yeah," Rosario says in a wounded voice. "Why didn't you tell us?"

"You super betrayed us," Kit says, stabbing her finger again. "You jammed up everything."

Wow. I feel very cornered by all these stabs and accusations. I squirm at little in my seat and feel the sharp points of the note in my pocket.

"I didn't know I wanted to be a clown until I suddenly did," I explain. That actually feels like the truth.

"Don't you feel sorry at all for dumping us with Pepper?" Kit asks.

"And what about lunch?" Heni adds. "We're supposed to be friends."

Rosario nods aggressively. Is there a way for me to win this argument? Should I just make up something crazy? Or is there an option I'm missing? The warning bell rings and I release a startled scream.

"What's wrong with you?" Kit asks.

"Yeah, why do you keep doing that?" Rosario adds.

Heni just stares at me with a face full of concern mixed with hurt. Behind her, in the hallway, Sasha, Frenchie, and Xander all wave to me. Imagine that, friends who wave instead of finger-stab. I'm so lucky to have met such generous eighth graders.

"Are you going to say anything?" asks Kit.

"I'm sorry tryouts felt wonky for you." I shrug. "And I hope we can move past it and enjoy the play."

"That's it? That's your apology?" Kit says with a voice full of disgust. "Not cool."

Wow. These kids hate me. Which I don't mind, but it would crush Old Poppy. Then I take out the note, which got really pocket-crumpled. Should I? Before I second-guess myself I cram it in Heni's hand. But I immediately regret this move, because what if the rest of the friendship glob wants to read it? What if Heni, a textbook pushover, shares it? That

CANNOT happen. I grab that note back, and shove it deep into my pocket again. Heni stares at her empty hand. Then she stares at me. Thankfully just then the start bell rings, I look down at my lap to stifle my scream, and the glob takes their seats. I can feel eyeballs crawling all over me.

If I were in a room with a bunch of other cats, nobody would be acting weird like this. We'd just be minding our own business, licking whatever we wanted to lick, and being chill.

Plop!

A note skitters across my desk. It has twenty exclamation marks on it.

Who wrote this thing? Did one of them pre-write me a note before class? How much time did these three kids put into this awful ambush? The piece of folded-up paper on my desk stinks of bad energy. Nothing in this note can be good. In fact, I'm worried it might actually contain a dead bug, so I just slip it into my pocket next to the other note. Old Poppy will totally flip out when I tell her about all this. I think I'm just gonna pretend none of it happened.

As I wait patiently for roll, I feel this weird tremble in my knee. I get them every now and then, sort of like a magical warning. But until recently I've always been a cat, so the tremble would signal something dangerous was nearby, like a dog or a vacuum or a four-wheeler. Why would my knee tremble in a fifth-grade classroom?

BEEP! BEEP! BEEP!

I release a shriek so pitched with fear that a random kid in the hallway opens the door to look at me. Then the intercom crackles to life and delivers an announcement so startling it stops my blood.

"UPPER TETON MIDDLE SCHOOL STUDENTS. THIS IS A FIRE DRILL. PLEASE FOLLOW YOUR TEACHERS' INSTRUCTIONS. FIRE WARDENS, PLEASE MOVE TO THE FRONT OF YOUR LINES AND LEAD YOUR GROUPS TO THEIR SAFETY ROUTES AND NEAREST EXITS. REMEMBER NOT TO RUN."

"Let's remain calm," Ms. Gish says. "It's the fire alarm. Everybody line up. Remember our evacuation plan."

OH. MY. BAT SNOT. THE. SCHOOL. IS. ON. FIRE.

I watch as the kids around me form a long, doomed line. It's as if I'm watching the emergency happen in slow motion. It makes no sense. They've just been told they're all about to die, and nobody is running for their lives.

But I'm no dummy. Old Poppy will be so proud when I tell her how I saved her life.

First, I bypass the line. Heni tries to grab me, insisting she's the "warden" and needs to count me, but I give her a solid "hi-yah!" and swat her away. Nothing can keep me in this classroom. I bolt out the door and then scream around a long line of kids exiting another room. I can't believe how calm they all look! They obviously don't know what's at stake.

But I do. Back when I was a kitten, before I ended up at the animal shelter and Poppy adopted me, I barely escaped a burning barn. Without three bold crows and a goat, I wouldn't be here now. The memory feels so real inside me, it's almost like it's happening again.

As I run I can hear people telling me to stop and slow down. It's bananas! I find myself operating on pure instincts. I feel so vulnerable. All I want is to know for sure that I'm safe. I do *not* want to die as a fifth grader.

119

As soon as I get outside underneath the bright sun, I dart toward an oak tree. At first, I hug it tightly and think I'll wait right here for my class.

But once the rough bark touches my skin, I'm overcome by an impulse to climb. To escape danger, cats are designed to go up. That feline gut reaction kicks in and I scramble up the trunk until I reach a sturdy limb and pull myself onto it. Repeat. Repeat. Repeat. By the time my class exits the building, I'm so high up in the tree that everybody looks small.

Unfortunately, they notice me right away. Apparently our classroom's safe zone was near the oak. They gawk at me in disbelief. I guess they're in shock that my instincts to live are so much stronger than theirs.

"Poppy McBean, come down from that tree right now," Ms. Gish sternly instructs.

That strikes me as a terrible idea. I look down at my teacher's squinty, worried face, and I hug this trunk tighter. I'm exactly where I want to be.

CHAPTER 8

Turtle Drama

Is Heni a normal friend? Is she a real friend? Is her heart
as soft as mine?

Those are the questions I'm struggling with while I
spend a huge chunk of the day all by myself on the counter,
nibbling small delicious tunnels through a loaf of pumpkin
bread. If she's a real friend, who's normal *and* healthily soft-
hearted, she'll find a way to forgive me. Real friends do that
for each other.

Then again, what if she reads my note and learns
about the curse and it changes how she feels about me?
What if she busts up our four-year bond over my terrible
(not-really-my-fault) behavior and I need to find a new
friend? How will I do that in the middle of fifth grade,
where everybody already has friends?

Holding on tightly with my claws, I steady myself on the counter's edge. As I lose my balance and tumble-plunge downward, I notice I'm leaving little scratch marks everywhere. They're deep enough that I don't think Mom can polish them out. Then I land on all four paws thanks to the miracle of my tail. Okay, sometimes being a cat is amazing.

Over at my water bowl, I check my reflection. Because I still feel like myself, I keep expecting to see my own face. Instead, I'm faced with a circle of fur with triangular ears, tiny pink lips, and long, stiff whiskers. It's unbelievable. How can this be me?

I try so hard not to think about school, but the worry eats at me. I mean, Heni has to believe me *and* forgive me, or my life will be so different and terrible that it won't even feel like my life. If she rejects me, all the kids at school will probably assume there's something wrong with me. Deezil will definitely start an extra mean rumor about me.

Heni and I have never talked about curses, but I want to believe that she's the kind of person who could understand them. And I hope after she learns the whole crazy truth that she's still able to remember the good stuff between us:

throwing pennies into the wishing well at the zoo, steering her toboggan down snowy hills, picking out organic lip gloss together at Fred Meyer.

Trying to solve fifth-grade problems with a walnut-size brain has wrecked me. Dizzily, I wobble toward my mother's sweater shelf in the back of her closet. Taking a marathon nap in her soft smell might relax and possibly repair me.

Dingy. Dong. Dingy. Dong.

Does this mean no nap? I redirect my wobbly walk to the front window. Using the last of my energy I lift myself to the ledge to see who's here.

"Hello? Hello? Is anybody home?"

Bummer. It sounds like Aunt Blanche got here early. I leap into the window to double-check. Bummer confirmed.

"Well, I didn't expect to see you here," she says, peering at me with a small frown. "Poor trapped fur baby."

It's weird that she sounds unhappy to see me. Due to his exceptional fluffiness, people usually enjoy encountering Mitten Man. I watch as Aunt Blanche struggles to remove a small potted tree from her car. She heaves it across the yard and then steadies it on the front step. It appears to be

123

a lemon tree roughly the same size as Big Poppy. Then she gathers two suitcases. We've never had a visitor bring two suitcases and a potted citrus tree before.

How long does she think she's staying?

She sits down next to the potted tree and whips out her phone. I stay in the window to see if I can figure out her plans.

"Marlena?" Aunt Blanche says. "I made it to the house early. I'm on the front step."

"An incident? At school? The fire chief?" Aunt Blanche says. "Well, don't worry about me. I'm fine here. I'll use the spare key and settle in."

Of course I'm deeply alarmed to hear that there was an incident at my school. Fridays are usually such good days for me. I hope it's something small. Maybe the incident doesn't even involve a real-life fire chief. Maybe they're talking about a movie called *The Incident at School with the Fire Chief*.

My brain already feels too crammed with worry, so I'm just going to pretend that's the truth until Big Poppy tells me differently.

It doesn't take Aunt Blanche long to enter the house, even with her tree and two suitcases, which she sets down right next to my kibble bowl.

"Oh, Mitten Man," Aunt Blanche says, and her voice is dripping with true tragedy. "Do you understand that you're a hostage?"

I can't tell if she's talking to me or her plant.

"I got you that collar to free your soul," she says. "But maybe I should free your whole being?"

Weird. I didn't realize that Aunt Blanche liked to have deep philosophical conversations with my cat when I was at school. "Let me get Ms. Lemon situated first. She needs a south-facing window and probably more rose quartz. I'm worried about her root vigor and gas transport."

Wow. When did Aunt Blanche become an expert in plant gas?

"Don't get too comfortable, you regal kitty. I'm about to change your life."

Yikes. Not only is Aunt Blanche totally oblivious that I'm stuck inside my cat, what she's saying sounds a little creepy. Is she speaking in code? As I take a step down the hallway toward her, there's this weird tremble in my right knee, but I ignore it and walk right up to Aunt Blanche, rubbing against her pant leg and sniffing her bags. Once I get past the initial odor of spices, I pick up all kinds of scents: lavender soap, black licorice, brand-new underwear elastic, a box of peppermints, a strong whiff of sandalwood, and yes, pickles.

"I think I'll unpack my things in Poppy's room," Aunt Blanche says. "Better energy in there. And her bed is so much cozier than the foldout couch in the office."

That's bad news for Big Poppy. In addition to the lumpy couch, the office currently has two buzzy flies in it. I'll have to warn her about them when she gets home.

Now, I follow behind Aunt Blanche to make sure she doesn't snoop through any of my things. She's like that. I need to remind Big Poppy to empty her trash every day, because Aunt Blanche will most definitely pick through it for bottles or some other random thing she's figured out how to recycle. All of a sudden, my knee starts trembling again. Why—

"Gotcha!" Aunt Blanche cheers as she flips around, grabs me roughly by the scruff of my neck, and dangles me over my bed. "I can feel your untamed heart," she purrs. "You want freedom and a life filled with adventure. And I want that for you too."

The way Aunt Blanche pinches the skin behind my neck makes my whole body go limp, and I can't break free. She carries me out of my bedroom. I can't believe she's going to toss me into the garage for no reason. I mean, I was behaving like a perfectly good cat!

But Aunt Blanche doesn't take me to the garage. She takes me to the front door.

"Now that you've got your moonstone collar, it's time for you to go out into the world and live the natural and rugged life you were always meant to! Namaste and bye-bye!"

When she slams the door shut, I'm shocked! What's wrong with her? I don't belong outside.

Caw. Caw.

A *gigantic* crow swoops down near my head and cries into my ear. Aah! I race around the side yard, past the woodpile, to the back door. Hanging out in the garage is way better than getting attacked by loud birds or worse. But when I get to the garage door, I find it shut and probably locked. Where is a safe place for a cat to hide until her owner gets home from school?

Just then, I hear a crunching noise in the grass behind me. I spin around. Oh no! Death Tiger pounces. He's on me! His big paws push me to the ground, his sharp teeth bite at my neck fur, and I can smell his terrible breath, stinky like ditch water and dead mice.

Nothing in my life has prepared me for this moment. I'm so freaked out that I release a low, crazy sound from somewhere deep inside my gut, a howl so terrible and weird that Death Tiger actually halts his attack.

"What's wrong with you?" he says.

And I'm off!

I motor as fast as a speedboat into Heni's yard. Unfortunately Death Tiger is apparently as fast as a cheetah. I don't have a good plan, so I race to the Kanoas' sliding glass door. If they see me, maybe they'll recognize me and rescue me before Death Tiger makes me an afternoon snack. I fling my paws onto the glass, dragging my claws to make a sound so hideous that I pull my paws away—and now Death Tiger's pouncing again. This time he hooks his teeth in my collar and drags me off the Kanoas' cement patio and into a bush.

I should have owned a fish. I can't believe my life will end this way. All I wanted was to be a dancing show pony with my friends, and now I'm about to die a very slashy death as a cat in my neighbor's creeping gardenias.

"If you don't bite my head, I won't bite yours!" I scream. Do I really have what it takes to bargain with a beast?

Maybe. Because just like that, instead of tearing me to ribbons or biting the life out of me, Death Tiger just pulls his head back and looks at me, one paw on my chest. I know if I try to escape, he'll easily catch me, so I stay motionless.

"You're so dramatic," Death Tiger says. "One day we have a plan to look for Raul, and the next day you act like we're not even friends anymore."

O-*kay*. . . . That's not what I expected Death Tiger to say. He thinks we're friends? How is that possible? Why would

Big Poppy tell me that I needed to avoid Death Tiger because he's a total beast and terminator if they're actually really friends?

"Uh . . . I've been feeling a little mixed up," I say. Which is the truth, because I can't believe my cat lies this much, especially to me, about important things.

"Well, get it together," Death Tiger says. "You know we need your A game."

I don't even know what to say. Part of me feels like I should explain to Death Tiger that I'm actually a fifth grader. But another part of me feels like that's probably the wrong move. He already thinks I'm too dramatic. Why would he even believe such a crazy story?

"Do you realize how bad things are?" Death Tiger says. "Raul has vanished. Poof!"

Death Tiger sounds so concerned that I start paying attention.

"Don't you feel guilty?" he says, sounding genuinely interested. "You're the reason all this happened."

I blink. It's hurtful to feel blamed when the real me didn't do anything wrong.

"You said you'd come up with a search plan," he continues. "You knew Raul better than any of us. You said he'd be easy to find and that you'd take us to Carl's sweet farm!"

"And I . . . still want to do that," I say, trying to absorb the whole unfolding story. Do I know anybody named Carl? With a farm? Is it possible my cat was living a secret life? "So where's the last place we saw Raul again?"

"He was living in your garage!" Death Tiger snaps. "It was the safest place, you said."

"Right," I say, pretending I'm not at all surprised to learn that a turtle named Raul recently lived in my garage. I know Mitten Man mentioned Raul, but why put him in our garage? What am I missing? Why would Big Poppy tell me one tiny piece of a story and leave all the important stuff out?

"So what's the plan now?" Death Tiger asks.

"First, like I always say, let's calm down," I tell him calmly, trying to buy time.

"You never say that!" Death Tiger shoots back at me.

A line of ants treks across the damp dirt between us, carrying crumbs of food back to their nest. When I listen closely, I realize they're making tiny sounds. It's like a chorus of chatter that feels almost like a melody. Once I start listening I almost can't stop.

"Hello?" "Obstacle." "Follow me." "Over it." "Around it." "Faster." "Through it." "Lift it." "Where?" "Here." "Higher." "Carry it home!"

Can Death Tiger hear the ants? Then again, do I really think Death Tiger is the sort of cat who's interested in bug conversations? Nope.

Death Tiger lowers his head and sniffs the ground. "Do you smell that?"

I sniff hard. Definitely there are some cows nearby.

"Weasels," Death Tiger says. "Death is in the air."

Wow. Things sure got bleak fast. My mind flashes back to poor Princess Tofu and the lost cat signs plastered throughout my neighborhood. It never occurred to me she might have been eaten by weasels. The outdoors are so much more dangerous than I realized.

Death Tiger releases a very mean growl.

"Was that to scare off the weasels?" I ask.

"No!" He glares at me. "I'm growling at you. You are a terrible friend. All your promises are worthless."

It hurts to have these things said right to your face, even if it's not really your own face. I feel awful that Death Tiger thinks that way about Mitten Man. An idea pops into my head.

"That's not true at all. Here's my plan," I say. "My owner's going to help us." It's time for Big Poppy to show up and fix things.

"What?!" Death Tiger yelps. "That's a horrible plan! You complain about that wishy-washy kid nonstop. She won't be a good turtle rescuer. Just yesterday she tried to chase me down in front of your house for no reason. She's a maniac!"

What did that cat just say? My brain feels split open. Why would *my* cat say these things about *me* to another cat? Mitten Man loves me with his whole heart. I stare at Death Tiger. He comes across as a very earnest cat. But why should I trust a random cat over my own eyeballs? I refuse to accept that my entire relationship with my cat has been a lie.

It really bothers me that this cat hates me. "It's just that she's very tall and has . . . arms. She'll be helpful in locating and rescuing a slow-moving animal." I mean, I don't have another plan.

Death Tiger hisses in disagreement. "We need somebody who's willing to risk everything. Climb fences. Trespass. Outsmart everyone, even that bully Whip. Will *she* do all that?"

What a negative cat. I don't know why Death Tiger thinks we're going to have to do all that stuff. He seems to have an excellent sense of smell. We might find Raul right away. "Of course!" I blurt out, "If there's one thing I know for certain, it's that you can always count on Poppy McBean." I really want to believe this is true.

Death Tiger gives me what can only be described as a death-y stare. "We're talking about your owner, right? The girl with the wet-looking, shiny clothes and smelly shoes?"

"That's Poppy, all right," I say, mustering up a bunch of pretend courage.

I need to tell Death Tiger what he wants to hear so that he'll stick with me while we're stuck out here. Everything is starting to get dark. Night will be here soon. What happens when the darkness swallows me?

CHAPTER 9

Thief Watch

Me and Marlena are sitting outside a house spying on it.
For her *job*. And she hasn't even complained that I've taken
off my shoes and stretched my socked feet onto the sunny
dashboard. Pretty cool afternoon. And now that Don's gone
all geo-trivia-obsessed on me, I'm on the lookout for a new
favorite parent.

"I'm impressed by your climbing skills, but deeply disappointed in your fire safety behavior," she says, lifting a pair
of binoculars to her eyes to inspect a mud-covered motor
home down the block.

"I contain multitudes," I say.

"Wow. I didn't expect to field that excuse until you were
a teenager."

I shrug. She must not like that response because she
sighs in a disappointed way, sets the binoculars down in

her lap, and turns to look at me with an intensity I haven't seen before.

"Listen, Poppy, I don't totally blame you for what happened at school today. I'm a private investigator. I get what's going on here."

"You do?" I ask.

But nope. "Dad and I shifted our attention away from you, and now you're acting out," she says.

Aaaand we're back to parent logic. What's the point of having a mom as a detective if she can't figure out that her daughter is actually a cat?

"It's natural. I get it. But now that Aunt Blanche is here, I expect things to normalize."

"Huh," I say. I don't expect having Aunt Blanche in our house will have that effect at all.

Marlena lifts the binoculars back to her eyes. "We're on the same page, right?"

People are so weird. If Marlena were really paying attention, she would see that we're not even reading the same book. But is it my job to fix the broken way she thinks? Nope.

"We're totally on the same page," I lie. It's just so much easier to tell her what she wants to hear. "Which one is the thief again?" I ask, trying to shift her attention away from me.

Marlena holds the binoculars with one hand and picks up a gigantic iced tea with the other. "The whole Gilligan family."

I probably should already know what's happened here, but to be honest, people problems bore me. I pull my feet off of the deliciously warm dashboard and open up my backpack to find some crackers. Oops. I feel terrible when I see Old Poppy's eclipse art getting squashed at the bottom. I really need to remember to turn that thing in.

"Pete Gilligan claims he has a back injury, and he's suing my client for an obscene amount of money."

I spot a robin in the tree beside the car. Geez, I would love to chase that thing and give it a good scare. Songbirds are so much fun to startle.

"And of course he hasn't really hurt his back. All the affidavits provided by his family are bogus. I need to get a few more seconds of video so I can prove all those statements are full of lies."

"So Pete's a liar and a thief," I say. "Not cool."

Marlena snaps a telescope lens onto her camera and films a man atop the motor home on his belly. Must be Pete. He reaches over the side, washing the windows with a tremendously long squeegee.

"His back looks stronger than mine," I say. "And look at that cool squeegee." If the McBeans had one of those and regularly cleaned all their windows with it, I could see neighborhood birds and my cat friends so much better. I make a note to mention this gift idea to Old Poppy.

Pete Gilligan climbs down a ladder on the back of the motor home and starts power-washing the tires.

"He has the energy level of a ferret," Marlena says. "The amount of dishonesty in that driveway disgusts me."

When a conversation starts feeling like a lecture about trustworthiness and other dull stuff, I try to change the subject. "So where are we taking Aunt Blanche for dinner?" I ask. I'll need to make sure to fix Old Poppy some toast *and* warn her about Aunt Blanche's dangerous, dark heart before we split for dinner. Too bad she's so thoroughly opposed to salmon pellets. My life would be so much simpler if she could just eat whatever gets left in the kibble bowl for her.

"Aunt Blanche wants to make us sesame soba noodles," Marlena says. She's stopped taking video and is now snapping photos of Pete as he dries the giant rig with a beach towel.

"That seems rude to make her cook right after she shows up," I say.

"Well, too late now," Marlena says. "She got in hours ago."

Oh my Buddha! It's as if somebody has thrown a bucket of pure dread on me. This can't be true. That woman with her bohemian ideas doesn't believe in indoor cats. She'll ambush Old Poppy as soon as she sees her. I have to get home!

"Oh, by the way. I need our toilet right now," I say. I figure this is the best fib to get Marlena moving quickly. "Not a store toilet. Not a gas station toilet. *Our* toilet." Lies don't count when you need a fast way to get home to stop an animal liberator from doing something reckless.

"Okay, sweetie." She eyes me, looking concerned. "Can you give me one quick minute?"

"No!" I scream. I'm so loud Pete looks down the block at us.

"Shh. Okay," she says, firing up the Jeep. "Let's keep a low profile, please."

I watch out the window as we zoom past people gardening and cows grazing in yellow-blossomed fields. I know there are other ways to live. Cities. Beach towns. Houseboats. What is it that makes people choose to spend their whole lives in a small Idaho town? If I could go anywhere, I'd probably venture to Egypt. They worship cats there. And because of the river culture, fish dinners are everywhere. Or maybe Paris would be a better fit. Or some place in Australia near the Sunshine Coast. I definitely would like to see more of the world than this.

I pop open my door as soon as we hit the driveway.

"Wait until we come to a complete stop!" Marlena yells.

"Next time!" I yell back. As soon as she slams the gear into park, I leap from the Jeep and run. As I enter the house, I catch the scent of Aunt Blanche: tree guts and antiseptic oils. It's shocking that that's all I can smell—usually, I catch a person's whole world in my nose. I guess a fifth grader's nostrils only capture the incredibly stinky parts.

"Hello?" I call, running to my room. Wow, Aunt Blanche's clothes are already everywhere and there's a weird dwarf citrus tree, possibly Lisbon, drooping big time in here. Holy dog butts. She's already started colonizing my space.

"Poppy McBean!" Aunt Blanche cheers. She has snuck up behind me, blocking the doorway to the hall. "Come over here and give your favorite aunt a hug."

The last thing I want to do is hug that wrongdoer. I stand still and let her clobber me with her arms.

"You've gotten so tall," she says. "You must be drinking lots of milk."

"I've recently had a tremendous growth spurt," I explain.

"And such a good vocabulary for an eleven-year-old," she says.

Marlena squeezes Aunt Blanche too. "Thanks for coming, B. It's so good to see you."

"Oh, it's a treat to spend time with this little devil," Aunt Blanche says. "She's my absolute favorite niece."

Wow. What nerve of this malicious lady to call Old Poppy a devil. Of all people! I try to keep my face from scowling too hard.

"Have you already used the bathroom?" Marlena asks.

"Mom!" That seems super rude to quiz me about in front of company. "I consider that question an invasion of privacy."

"It's the whole reason we drove home like we were on fire," she says, super confused.

Oh yeah. I forgot about that lie.

"Mitten Man!" I holler. I dive onto the floor and crawl on my hands and knees to check the hiding space in the back of the closet. Nothing. "I'm home!" I yell. Great, Old Poppy isn't anywhere. My stomach twists with worry in a way it never does except when something dire happens, like when I accidentally swallow a moth.

"Calm down," Aunt Blanche says. "I caught Mitten Man playing with the dirt in the begonia plant on the kitchen table so I put him in the garage. For kitties, digging is a natural territorial behavior."

Aunt Blanche is built out of lies! Old Poppy would never play around with the begonia dirt! I race to the garage. "I'm here! I'm home!" But I don't hear anything.

Horrible images flash through my mind. What if a skunk bites off her ears? What if a coyote chews up one of her

hind legs? How good could she possibly be at finding a water source *and* defending herself with three untrained legs
and one intact ear? Even on her best day she's not tactical
and lacks combat skills. Let's face it: Like duckling fluff or
cashmere yarn, Old Poppy's got an all-soft core. I notice cat
hair clinging to Aunt Blanche's pant leg. What did this fib-
ber do with our cat?

"Mitten Man has gotten out before," Marlena says.
"Calm down, Pops. I'm sure he'll be home soon. He's always
made it home for supper."

Basically, that's the worst idea ever spoken by a person
with a mouth.

"I bet I know where she is!" I say.

"Isn't Mitten Man a . . . *man* cat?" Aunt Blanche asks.

Ugh. I don't have time for dumb questions. I launch
myself full-speed toward Heni's house, because I know
that's what Old Poppy would do. She'd want her friend to
help her. But upon arriving at the sliding glass back door I
see something awful. Old Poppy's nose smears are all over
it. I bend down and smell the cement steps. Even with my
weak nose, I think I can smell Death Tiger too.

"Are you okay?" a voice asks.

"Augh!" I scream.

It's Heni. She's opened up her sliding glass door and stares at me with a very wrinkled face.

"My aunt Blanche put Mitten Man in the garage and he escaped and I thought he might have come here."

"I've only seen that big orange cat," Heni says.

"Uh, I think I know my own cat's nose smears when I see them."

Heni stares at me.

"And these are them!"

"Wow," she says. "They just look like dead bug squish marks to me."

That really offends me, but I try not to show it.

"How are you feeling?" Heni asks. "You looked really pale when you finally came down from that tree."

I cannot believe Heni brought up the tree fiasco. Clearly, we both know it wasn't my best moment. I mean, that ambulance showed up for no reason.

"I'm fine. Except for Mitten Man being loose," I say.

"Good. So . . . don't you want to ask me about the play?" Heni says. "They announced the parts."

It's hard for me to care about some piece of amateur theater knowing that my owner is fighting for her life in the rural outback with dusk fast approaching.

"I really need to look for my cat right now," I snap.

"Maybe I can help," Heni offers, pointing to a spot on her arm below a freckle. "I got my last shot. I should be fine now." *Achoo. Achoo.*

Gross. Some of Heni's wet sneeze just landed on my arm. I rub it on my leggings.

"Sweetie, we need to get home and have dinner," Marlena says, coming up behind me with Aunt Blanche. "If he's not home by the time dinner ends, we can form a search party."

Losing valuable time feels like a terrible mistake. Most missing people are found in the first twenty-four hours— and if they aren't found by then, they stay missing. Cats probably share a similar statistic. Shouldn't a detective know this? I bet that Marlena McBean wouldn't make such a rotten suggestion if she knew it was her only daughter out there all alone, thrust into the wilds of Idaho without any useful survival skills.

"Well, if you need help, I'm here," Heni says. "Just come and get me."

Ugh, Heni. Her infinite patience is driving me crazy. She gives me a soft smile and stares at me with genuine, concerned eyes.

"What a nice friend," Aunt Blanche says. "She looks like a doll and acts like one too."

Humans are so weird. Heni doesn't look or act anything like a doll. I watched a show on doll assembly and learned that most dolls are made out of odorless plastic, some of which is toxic when bitten or licked. So in addition to being part wicked hippie, Poppy's aunt is a terrible judge of character.

Before I can disagree with this terrible plan to give up, I hear the crunch of a small animal pouncing through the alfalfa field behind Heni's house. I flip around, but Poppy's mom grabs my arm.

"Stop!" Marlena yells. "You can't trample the hay fields. It'll ruin the crop!"

I notice how firm Marlena's voice sounds, and I get the feeling I need to do what she says.

"Hide in a safe place!" I yell into the hayfield at the top of my lungs. "Climb a tall tree or a swing set or a trampoline!

Whatever you do, don't approach a weasel, they'll kick your butt in an instant; they start their fights by eating your brains! I'll come find you after dinner!"

As I glumly turn around to head home I can feel Aunt Blanche, Marlena, and Heni looking at me like I've totally lost it. If they only knew the real truth, they'd drop their whole lives in an instant, trample any *crop* that stood in their way, and bring Old Poppy home safe where she belongs.

CHAPTER 10

A Dangerous Tail

"It looks like they're eating vegan food," I say, peeking in the sliding glass door from a bush beside the back patio.

"We should go check the asparagus patch. Look and see if Raul's there. That's where he was supposed to be before he vanished."

Wow. Death Tiger really does need somebody else to help him make plans. "If that's where he was when he truly vanished, he's not going to be there anymore," I explain. "In fact, a vanished turtle will be very hard to find, which is why we need Big Poppy." I re-aim my focus on watching my old self. I deeply miss pants.

"The girl doesn't seem too worried that you're missing," Death Tiger says. "I've seen her eat five meatballs."

"They're beanballs," I say under my breath. Aunt Blanche's diet has been nut and plant–based my entire life, so I know which dinners to dread when she comes over.

"Wow. That's even worse. She *really* doesn't miss you," Death Tiger says.

Death Tiger is starting to remind me of Kit. I bet she'd be making me feel bad about meatballs or beanballs too. But I'm really hoping that Big Poppy will know exactly where to find Raul. Maybe I won't even need to go on the search for him. Maybe Big Poppy can stash me in the warm house, then take Death Tiger and recover this lost turtle without me. Seriously, Raul isn't my friend, which means I don't know any of his hiding places. Whereas if it were Heni who had disappeared, I'd know to look for her in the decorated refrigerator box in her garage.

"Listen, the air keeps smelling more and more weaselly. We shouldn't leave Raul out there alone." Death Tiger follows my gaze. "There's no way they're snarfing that down in five minutes."

I keep trying to twist things in Big Poppy's favor. But if you look at the facts, if we reversed the situation, would I be sitting on a kitchen chair eating beanballs and a dairy-free fruit tart while my pet was outside lost in the wilderness? Of course not. I'd be out here with a flashlight, sweetly calling Mitten Man's name until I found him. What's wrong

149

with Big Poppy? Why aren't her heart and brain functioning together?

"Let's go!" Death Tiger snaps at me.

Just then we hear the sound of footsteps. It's Heni! She gently knocks on our glass door, and Big Poppy jumps out of her chair to open it.

"Hey," Heni says. "Just wondering if you're ready to look for Mitten Man."

Unexpected happiness hops around inside me. My best friend wants to help find me. Wait. If Heni were looking for me, would she really call me Mitten Man? Wouldn't she call me by my name? And wouldn't she alert my parents? It just doesn't feel like she's read the note.

"Yeah," Big Poppy says. "I am. Can I eat dessert after I get back?"

Okay, I want to believe that she loves me way more than a fruit tart. Even if she didn't give Heni that note.

"She cares about that fruit pile way more than you," Death Tiger says.

"Shut up," I hiss. Now Big Poppy, my parents, Heni, and Aunt Blanche are all exiting the house together. Big

Poppy sweeps the ground in front of her with the beam of a giant flashlight.

"Great, now that she's part of a mob, there's no way you'll be able to get her attention. And if her parents see you, they'll put you back in the house and I'll be right back where I started. Solving my problem alone. This is a lose-lose situation."

For somebody named Death Tiger, he sure whines a lot. But geez, I need for Big Poppy to prove to me in front of Death Tiger that she absolutely loves me and is loyal to the bone.

Heni stops walking. "Do you guys hear that? It sounds like a cat."

"I didn't hear anything," says Aunt Blanche.

"I thought it was an owl," Dad says.

"You girls wait by this mailbox while we check out those dark bushes," Mom says, swiping the flashlight from Big Poppy. "Definitely a good hiding place for something."

Yes! Got her alone. I smile smugly at Death Tiger.

"You really should never make that face again," Death Tiger says. "You look like a rude goat."

That was actually a pretty decent burn. I need to remember that one to use later in a note to Heni about Deezil. Or maybe even about Kit.

I know I need to act, but something stops me when I see Big Poppy standing beside Heni. I've never looked at my life from outside my body before. It's so weird. I see myself. I see my best friend. But it's like we're on different planets. I'm in a trance, watching them stare at each other, completely wordless.

"What are we waiting for?" Death Tiger asks.

"Shh!" My knee trembles, and I feel like I'm about to learn something so valuable that it could change my whole life. Maybe she's going to give her the note right now. Maybe this is the moment my life changes for the better.

"Things feel weird between us right now," Heni says. "And what I say next will probably make things feel much worse."

"Maybe you shouldn't say those things then," Big Poppy says, shoving her hands deep into her pockets, looking away from my friend. "I've got a lot on my plate right now."

I cannot believe this. I'm watching the only meaningful friendship I've ever had in my whole life fall apart in front of me.

"Well, I promised Kit and Rosario I'd tell you the news," Heni says. "You got the part. You're Runaway Clown."

Oh. My. God. Why do I have to be a ridiculous clown? And why do I have to learn such rotten news while crouching in a wet pile of leaves beside grasshoppers and a pine cone?

"Is there something else?" Big Poppy asks, looking up at Heni brightly. "Because that news hasn't worsened things."

"Well, not that you asked, but I'm a dancing pony," Heni says.

"Good," Big Poppy says. "So everybody got what they wanted."

Big Poppy sounds so disconnected from what Heni's telling her. Clearly, Heni is super upset. But Big Poppy doesn't seem to care at all. She should be acting more like a friend and reaching out to make Heni feel better.

"Ouch!" Aunt Blanche cries, in the back of the family pack. "Something big and heavy just stepped on my pinky toe."

"Was it your other foot?" Dad asks.

"We're wasting our lives *and Raul's too*," Death Tiger spits at me.

"One more minute. Please!" I hiss back. I don't feel like I can leave, not with Heni pouring out her heart.

153

"No, Poppy . . ." Heni sounds so disappointed in me. "We didn't all get the pony parts."

"Poor Rosario!" Big Poppy says. "Her stiff hips and wide feet were definitely obstacles."

I cannot believe that Big Poppy keeps insulting my friends. That was not the deal we made last night.

"Rosario and I are both ponies," Heni says sharply, looking less disappointed and more upset. "It's Kit. She has to be a dog."

"Wow!" Big Poppy says. "What a curveball."

"Here," Heni says. "This is from all three of us."

"No thanks," Big Poppy says. "I still haven't read the last note you guys gave me."

I can't even believe my ears. You can't refuse a note from your friend. That's basically declaring that you aren't even friends anymore. And what happened to the note Big Poppy and I wrote last night? That's what we should all be talking about!

"You have to take it," Heni says.

"Actually, I don't," Big Poppy says.

"I'm going to find Raul!" Death Tiger says.

He springs away, jumping into a wheat field. His leaps bend the grain down just enough to leave a trail. Of course I have to stay to see how Big Poppy turns this around. She's not going to let Heni end our friendship in a random driveway beside a ditch. After I see how this resolves, then I'll get Big Poppy's attention and we'll both follow Death Tiger.

"Poppy, you broke up our friendship clump," Heni says. "So now things are gonna be different. I'm sorry, but we don't want to eat lunch with you anymore."

How can Big Poppy just stand there? Why isn't she trying to fix this? I'm so nervous I hold my breath and my whole body tightens. But all she does is shrug. I'm stunned. Shocked. Sad. As I wait by myself in the darkness, under stars that don't even shine, I keep hoping for Big Poppy to have a regular reaction, something that will get my friends back on my side.

Everything good about my life is unraveling.

Uh oh. Now Big Poppy is walking right over to Heni so their sneakers touch. All at once I understand: Big Poppy doesn't want to fix anything for me. She doesn't care. Just then, I hear something beside me. It's a grasshopper,

155

making a soft clicking noise. They're words! I can understand grasshoppers too?

"This night is cold.

This night is dark.

It cloaks my head.

It slows my heart."

Is it weird to think that the grasshopper's song is sort of about me? I agree with all of it. Even the part about having a cloaked head and a slowed heart. When your best friend in the world dumps you and there's nothing you can do because you're actually a cat, even your internal organs feel the pain of things.

"If you were really my friend, you would never have left me on the hallway floor," Big Poppy says with a voice so full of spite it makes me shiver.

Turning into a cat was not the worst day of my life. Today is. As I watch Heni and think about my old life, the pain won't stop blooming inside me. My face. My heart. My tail. It just keeps growing and filling every piece of me. What will I do without Heni?

Then the hurt flips to anger. How dare Big Poppy treat my life and friends so shabbily! The girl standing before me who looks like me is a total monster. I leap from my hiding spot and yowl.

"Skunk!" Aunt Blanche screams as she stumbles backward.

"Weasel!" Death Tiger cries as he races back toward me.

This seems impossible. Is Idaho so dangerous that there's a skunk and a weasel and me in the same place at the same time? Being a cat in the wilderness reminds me of playing dodgeball, but instead of balls, the world throws sharp-toothed, hungry animals at you.

"The night hides what the night hides," a grasshopper chirps.

"The night hurts what the nights hurts," a second grasshopper responds.

I'm so overwhelmed that instead of leaping into action I stay hunkered down.

"Safe in a bush, unless you die in a bush."

"Stop chirping terrible things about my life!" I tell the grasshoppers. But where am I supposed to go?

Death Tiger jumps toward me, eyes frenzied with fear.

I should have listened to him. We should have left earlier. As if to confirm my regret, an actual skunk sprints across the ground.

"Just keep backing away," Aunt Blanche says. "She'll only spray us if we scare her."

"Are you sure? Look at that dangerous tail!" Mom says.

The fluffy skunk toddles toward them, tail high, but not squirting its terrible stink—yet.

"Run!" Mom yells.

"Follow me!" Death Tiger howls.

And to my surprise my instinct is not to run toward Big Poppy and Heni and all of my life—I leap in the exact opposite direction. I follow Death Tiger.

So much is happening all at once, and I feel confused by a lot of it. As I race behind him I notice a dark trail of dots. It's blood. Who's bleeding?

"Mitten Man!" Heni cries. "*Achoo!* There goes Mitten Man! In that driveway!"

"Catch her!" Big Poppy cries.

"Faster!" Death Tiger hollers at me.

"Poppy!" Big Poppy screams.

Her voice makes my fur bristle. We are definitely no longer on the same team. I'm beginning to understand how much she's taken me for granted. Why race into the arms of a person I can't trust? Why not stay out here? I think Death Tiger might be hurt. I mean, I could help him and at the same time I could teach ungrateful Big Poppy a lesson. Maybe I don't even need Big Poppy's help to change back. I'm the one with the collar. I'm the one who goes to middle school and, if I count kindergarten, the one with more than five years of science. Why do I need Old Poppy to save me?

As I rush across white clover and through knapweed, I know that nothing will ever be the same. It's like for the first time in my life, I've finally opened my eyes.

CHAPTER 11

I'm Likable

Why would Old Poppy run away from me like that? It makes no sense. She doesn't belong outside with these animals. She belongs inside with me, Don, Marlena, and her terrible Aunt Blanche. What's she thinking? When does she plan on coming home?

This night has been a complete catastrophe. If I had my old nose, I would have been able to smell all the danger before it found me. But tonight, everything snuck up on me from behind. Even Heni. As I walk back home beside her, I'm surprised not only that she's throwing in the towel on our friendship, but that it bothers me. I've only known her for a couple of days, but to dump me completely feels harsh. I know I haven't been a perfect friend, but it's not like I did anything super unforgivable like bite off one of her ears.

As we approach our street, Heni's on the verge of tears. "Why are you acting so different?"

I'm not sure the truth would help where we've ended up, so I keep my mouth shut. Why should I be the one to fix all this? She's the one who gave me a break-up note and made her sad announcement. My parents and Aunt Blanche walk a little bit ahead of us. I don't know if they know we're fighting, or if they're just giving us space to talk.

"Aren't you going to say anything?" Heni asks.

"Well, everything that just happened with my cat is super upsetting," I say.

"I mean about us! About what I just told you!"

I wait a second or two before I answer, so she'll think I've thought about what I'm saying, when really, I don't know what a person is supposed to say at a moment like this. I'm still a little concerned we're going to run into another skunk. "Let's face it, Kit has a mean streak. Eating with the eighth graders will be fun. It's a win-win. I don't lose anything."

Uh-oh. I can see two big tears now. I didn't mean to do that. She sniffles and wipes them away with the back of her jacket.

"You lose *me*," she says.

Oops. I feel like she set a trap and I walked right into it. Heni is smarter than she looks. I glance at her. It's very weird-feeling, knowing that you're making a person cry. Maybe if I don't say anything else she'll stop.

"Before you changed and became totally different, I was thinking maybe we should start eating lunch together." She keeps going. Talking *and* crying. Darn. "Just us, I mean. I was thinking of how we could do it without hurting anybody's feelings. I . . . kind of know what you mean about Kit." She sounds like she's admitting to kidnapping.

Is this another trap? I can't tell. I see more tears. Maybe Heni really does feel this way. But what about Old Poppy's feelings? Heni and that glob put her through so much hurt.

But she's gently shaking her head. "Not anymore, though. I never knew how little you cared about us," Heni says. "One day you're going to regret throwing your friends away like this."

I've never been so happy to arrive at our lawn.

"He must not have recognized us," Don's saying.

"We might have spooked him with the flashlight," Marlena says.

"I'm sure he'll tumble back home in one piece," Aunt Blanche says. "If he so chooses. He has the whole world at his paws now. And cats are born with a million great instincts. They really are resilient little beasts."

I doubt she really cares whether Old Poppy tumbles home or not. Tonight has been too much for me. I wasn't built to navigate the emotional needs of eleven-year-olds and pretend to be nice to a phony aunt on the same day. It's time for me to say cheerio to all my problems. "Good night, everybody. I'm going to bed."

I don't wait for anybody to give me permission to leave. I walk into the house and collapse on the terrible couch/bed. I'm sure Old Poppy recognized me. We were so close. Why wouldn't she let me pick her up? Why wouldn't she want to come home? My mind sorts through the reasons. Maybe she's injured. That's happened to me before. I've taken a knock to the head and my ears ring and it takes me a few seconds to remember everything.

But we were out there longer than a few seconds. I think she was actually avoiding me. Why would she do that? I'm so nervous that I can't stop biting my bottom lip. When I was a cat I never did that because I didn't have chewable lips. *Nibble. Nibble.* She'll come back, right?

Based on what I've learned about fifth graders, they like getting notes. I pull a spiral notebook out of my backpack. Where do I start? Wait. Can Old Poppy still read words? When she helped me write the notes for Heni she didn't actually spell any of it. Plus, she's able to understand Death Tiger's meows, and when he crossed our path just now, I couldn't understand any of his meows. It feels like the longer I stay in Poppy's body the more of a person I become. I mean, I actually care about Heni Kanoa's feelings. That's not normal for me at all. Maybe the same thing is happening to Old Poppy. Maybe the longer she stays in my body, the less she is of herself.

Holy cougar farts. That makes sense. Maybe she's turning into an actual cat. Maybe that's why she didn't come to me.

What happens if Old Poppy forgets who she is entirely? Will that mean we won't be able to communicate anymore? At the top of the paper I scribble: *CAN YOU UNDER-STAND ME?* Then I grab a red checker from the game corner. I write the words *YES* and *NO* at the bottom of the page. When Old Poppy comes back I'll make her answer this question every morning. I'll start tracking her Old

Poppy–ness levels and figure out if they're declining. Unless that involves knowing fractions?

Knock. Knock.

I really hope that's not Aunt Blanche.

"It's Aunt Blanche. Can I come in?"

"No," I say, stashing my notebook under the bed. I know that's rude, but I just can't deal with her right now.

Knock. Knock. Knock.

"Now it's Dad and Aunt Blanche. Can we come in?"

Who can say no to Don? Not me. "Okay."

Aunt Blanche, Marlena, and Don wander in and look at me with so much pity I have to close my eyes.

"Let's focus on the positive," Aunt Blanche says. "That cat ran away from us so fast there's no way he's seriously injured."

My mouth drops open. Why is she such a drag?

"What Aunt Blanche probably means is that it's good he looks unharmed," Marlena says quickly.

"And it seems like he's made friends with that other cat," Don says.

"*I'm* his friend," I correct. "He needs to come home."

Per usual, Marlena flips into analytical mode. "Let's turn to past behavior to predict what will happen. Mitten Man has run away before, and he's always come home in one piece."

Don comes and sits beside me on the bed/couch. His weight next to me makes me lean toward him. "Your mom's right," he says. "He's probably having the time of his life."

I feel like crying. If they only knew how bad things really were, they'd call the police and we'd form a giant search party. Probably with ten thousand bloodhounds and a psychic. Old Poppy doesn't have survival instincts. Based on everything I know about her, it's safe to say that she's the most vulnerable cat in the world.

CHAPTER 12

The Warning Signs

I can't believe I'm really doing this. My fur feels electric. I thought I'd feel weighed down by fear, totally scared to leave everybody behind. But I feel buzzy and excited. For the first time in forever, I'm doing something that I want to do, something that actually matters, and not just following the glob. I am going to save an actual animal. Possibly more than one. And maybe I don't need to worry about that blood I saw earlier, because it's stopped appearing. Maybe I got so scared I imagined it. Maybe nobody is injured.

Every time we slow down and I think we've reached our destination, Death Tiger keeps moving, weaving quickly through tall weeds. When we finally stop beside a large tree, Death Tiger claws his way to a tall branch. I stay on the ground, remembering Mom's Eastern Idaho State Fair rooster plate.

"What do you see?" I ask.

Death Tiger doesn't answer, just cracks open his mouth and inhales deeply. So I do the same. And hey, I can smell something! It's metallic. Like a paperclip. And also earthy. Death Tiger drops hard from the tree. Did he fall? He stays low, belly dragging in the dirt, and inches himself into a bush.

"What did you see?" I ask.

But instead of answering, he whimpers. As I approach him, I notice bright red smears on the tall grass and leaves. I was right. He's been hurt this whole time.

"You're not okay," I tell him. "You shouldn't run anymore."

His fluffy face is pinched with pain. "He didn't get me that bad."

"Who?" I ask. "The weasel?"

"Yes," Death Tiger says, wincing.

"Where did he get you?" I ask. Maybe it's a very superficial wound, like the tail or an ear.

"On the leg. Coming back from the asparagus patch."

I feel guilty. If I'd gone with him instead of lingered to spy on the traitorous Big Poppy, would that attack have even happened? Could I have tried harder to talk him out of going? I ignored his weasel warning completely—more than once. I never realized cats were so unprotected outdoors at night until I became one. If I could change places with this injured orange mini tiger, I would do it in an instant. I feel such deep regret. After I help him recover, I hope a lot of this guilt simply floats away.

"I'll stay with you," I tell him. "You need to rest now. And then once you're better, we'll rescue Raul."

"I'm fine," he says, not even looking at me.

I walk over to join him as he curls up, hidden in the grass. I press my belly against his back.

"When there's sunlight we can go find fresh water," I say. "Then we'll both look for food. Then Raul. In that order."

"Good plan," he says. His voice is almost a whisper. He hasn't shown me his leg. Maybe it isn't that bad. Maybe we will be able to do all these things.

I tuck my head into Death Tiger's neck fur. I never thought I would live a day that would end with so much injury and betrayal. Still, I know things will get better because I'll *make them* better. I can do that now, as a cat.

Death Tiger tosses his tail over my legs, and the warmth that we make together begins to relax me. I hear the sound of him starting to purr. Then I feel my own voice box rumble.

169

As my muscles loosen, I start to drift. Even though I'm a cat buddy-napping in a field with another cat, it's the closest I've gotten to feeling like myself in a long, long time.

• • • • •

I wake up to the chatter of grasshoppers leaping into the bunchgrass around me.

"*We like to eat green leafy things.*

We hide our ears beneath our wings.

We rub our legs to make our song.

We're sad we can't live all year long."

I cock my ears as they leap away into the field behind us.

"*Nibble. Nibble. Time goes fast.*

Nibble. Nibble. Nothing lasts."

"What do you hear?" Death Tiger asks me.

"Just the grasshoppers," I say.

Death Tiger twists his mouth into an angry snarl.

"Why are you listening to them?" he rasps. "You know their game."

Actually, I do not. Are cats and grasshoppers natural enemies and I somehow went my whole life without knowing this?

"Why tempt them?" Death Tiger continues. "Once they get inside your head, they stay there, chirping about

170

misfortune, suffering, and danger. Their songs will make you doubt your best instincts."

Wow. Death Tiger thinks that grasshoppers are evil-hearted mind-controllers. As someone who has lived as a human for most of my life, it's hard for me to see that. Sometimes Heni and I try to catch grasshoppers with our bare hands in the grass. They're harmless.

"When you listen to the grasshoppers, you put us in danger," Death Tiger says. "Got it?"

"Sure," I say. But I'm not sure I should trust every word that Death Tiger says. He's lost one slow-moving friend and doesn't even know my true identity. So I'm not sure he's the genius he thinks he is.

Death Tiger's mean glare softens and he looks like a normal-faced, even-tempered cat again. "We're not far from backyards. If we can get there safely, we can go get food. We'll try the bird feeder at the yellow house."

"Are you feeling well enough to do that?" I ask.

Death Tiger lifts his hind leg and gives it several quick licks. "I need to get something to drink."

For the next little while, I'm just going to pretend I'm part of the glob again and agree with everything Death

171

Tiger says to smooth things over. I can't exactly name it, but there's something about Death Tiger that I like. I think I prefer his company over Kit's. "Roger that," I say.

"Who's Roger?" Death Tiger asks. "Is that the new indoor cat at the blue house?"

"No. It's just something I heard my owner say once," I say. "It means, like, *I'm okay with your idea.* There is no cat named Roger. I mean, I'm sure somewhere there's a cat named Roger, I've just never met him."

Death Tiger shoots me his death-y stare again and I stop talking. Every time a grasshopper jumps across my path, I try not to listen to it and stay focused on Death Tiger and his long, orange, curvy tail.

I'm actually excited. Normally nibbling on seeds from a bird feeder would gross me out, but my belly feels so empty. I've decided that I'm even willing to eat seeds off the ground. I'm prepared to swallow that birdseed if I've got to knock ants off it.

Looks like we're going to have competition. There are already magpies, robins, and a lone gray squirrel trying to grab seeds from the bird feeder at the yellow house. The squirrel takes a leap and clings with his tiny claws to the edge of the feeder's bottom bronze dish. Desperate times here, it seems.

I study Death Tiger. When he pounces, I'll pounce. There's a nice pile of seeds underneath the feeder. One hungry magpie stands on top of the small mound, devouring it.

It's like I can predict Death Tiger's pounce. Even with a hurt leg, as fast as lightning, he launches toward the seed pile with the magpie on it. I join him, wondering if we'll transport the seed heap to a safer spot or eat it right here.

But Death Tiger's not after the seeds! He leaps upward as the magpie takes flight, his claws slicing through the air, and catches the bird's tail feather and claws the magpie back to the ground.

I'm stunned. So is the bird. It opens its dark beak and releases a squawk so loud I put my paws over my ears. Death Tiger claws at it viciously, but the bird flaps backward out of his grasp, and all the robins and the other magpies take flight. I totally get what's happening now. What a great plan. We'll be able to eat all the seeds without any competition!

"What's wrong with you?" Death Tiger scolds.

I keep gobbling up birdseed. Am I doing this wrong too?

"You ruined our best chance at a hot breakfast!"

Wait a minute. We're supposed to eat the *birds*?? Death Tiger looks ruthless, claws out and mouth open. He's the most savage animal I've ever seen.

Just then a screen door swings open and a woman wearing a lavender bathrobe screams at us.

"Run!" Death Tiger says, and bolts.

Maybe it's because until recently I was a person, but I'm not terrified of the woman. Even as she lifts a spray bottle and takes aim at me, I try to eat a few more seeds. *Spritz! Spritz!*

"Get him again!" somebody yells.

I look up. There are now two women in bathrobes squirting water at me. Uh-oh. It smells funny.

"Teach it a lesson!" the second woman screams. "Outdoor cats cause bird decline!"

I race as fast as I can to a fence. Several more squirts hit my head and sides. The squirting women race closer. Is it possible that I could get squirted to death? Out of nowhere, Death Tiger appears on the other side of the fence.

"This way!" he cries.

I hurl myself through the opening, pressing my whiskers all the way back to my ears, sprinting after Death Tiger until we reach a grove of pine trees on the other side of the field. We collapse on the grass and breathe hard. There is a stink embedded in my fur that turns my stomach.

"Did they shoot me with poison?" I ask.

Death Tiger glares at me. "They shot you with cat repellent. You're the one who explained the ingredients of that stuff to me. Remember? Water, apple cider vinegar, citronella, sometimes passion flower."

Cat repellant. That makes sense.

"Should I lick it off?" I ask.

He moves in so close I can feel his moist nose touching my nose. "There's something seriously wrong with you."

I wasn't expecting him to confront me to my face like this. In fifth grade, if you have a problem with somebody, you talk about that person with your friends for weeks. Then, after everybody else knows about your problem, you feel better. And you never even need to tell the person you had a problem with what's wrong. Death Tiger's face-to-face questioning has thrown me for a loop.

Death Tiger walks around me in a circle, inspecting me. "You look normal, but you're acting bizarre. Why?"

I panic-blink. Seriously, I can't stop opening and closing my eyes. "I ate some ants in the garage last week. Mutant ants, I think. They had more than six legs, for sure. Maybe that's the problem. Hey, guess what I feel like doing right now? Throttling some birds to death. Let's go!" I truly hope all the birds I come across today are faster than my paws. I try to take the lead so that Death Tiger will follow me, but that doesn't happen. He actually bites my tail and tugs me back.

"I just risked my butt to save your butt from stink sprayers after you scared away my bird," Death Tiger grumbles.

I'm not ready to risk telling anybody the truth about who I am or why I'm "bizarre." No sir. It's time for me to go full Mitten Man on this cat. I gently grab his tail in my mouth and tug. "How many times do you want me to thank you? I mean, how many times have I saved your butt? And do I constantly bring it up? No! Because that's what friends do! Save butts!"

I conclude by lunging toward this small pond we ended up near. That's what Mitten Man would do. Wow. Before this moment, I never knew such a delicious small pond existed in my neighborhood. Maybe after I turn back into a fifth grader I should explore more. Who knows? Maybe I'm built for watersports and I haven't even tried them. All I know now is I *LOVE* this water.

Whoops. Death Tiger's watching the way I drink. I erase the happiness from my face and scowl at my surroundings.

"So for the last time, thanks for saving my butt. You owed me," I growl. "Now can we stop complaining and find something else to eat!"

"Fine," he says, practically collapsing next to the pond.

He stretches his leg out and I see the dark red wound. If it doesn't get infected, it will heal. If it does get infected, we're in trouble. We live in the dirt. Drink water wherever we find it. Bugs crawl on us when we're awake and asleep. Is it really possible to avoid bacteria under these conditions without any bandages or Neosporin?

Grasshoppers chirp beside me and I listen.

"Things will not go well tonight.

The list grows long for what you'll fight."

Why do I get the feeling that these grasshoppers know something I don't?

CHAPTER 13

Cookie Trick

Wishing things are different doesn't change anything, no matter how big your brain happens to be. I wished for three days that Old Poppy would return home. Nothing. I wished for three days that the friendship glob would apologize to me for being so weird. Zilch. I wished for three days that Aunt Blanche would leave our house and return to her own. And yet she remains here. Currently, she's at our breakfast table. Ruining the fun family mornings I was about to grow to love.

"This smells wonderful," Marlena says, inhaling the steam as it rises off her gooey plate.

"My friend Marwa taught me how to make it. I mean, who doesn't love paprika, cilantro, pasture-raised eggs, and warm tomatoes?"

"Shakshuka," Don says. "Am I saying it right?"

"Sure," Aunt Blanche replies, scooping a giant wad of it onto a piece of toast for me.

"I usually don't eat tomato-based foods before school," I explain.

"Mmm," Don says, taking a giant bite. "You'll love this, Poppy."

How quickly your fortunes can turn. It only took a few days to go from fluffy pancakes to watery eggs.

"The shakshuka is only my first surprise of the day," Aunt Blanche says. "Time for a little something I bought Poppy from Australia. I hope it cheers you up, dear heart."

"When did you go to Australia?" Marlena asks.

Aunt Blanche brushes past the question. "Inspired by Australia," she clarifies.

And then, because she's not at all normal, instead of handing me a package to unwrap, she thrusts a naked T-shirt at me and squeals, "I know you'll love it!"

The shirt feels soft, which is good, but instead of being a good color it's a cross between poop brown and puke green. I don't have any idea what's on it. It looks like two blobby animals with poorly drawn facial features wrestling each other. Also, the neck has a bunch of hot-pink crystals glued to it. Super bizarro.

"Wow!" Marlena says. "That's so thoughtful."

"Are those some sort of Australian animals?" Don asks.

"It's custom made. It's a picture of Poppy and a whiptail wallaby. I used the Christmas postcard you sent to make it. So they used her actual image! Isn't it fetching?"

Aunt Blanche has always struck me as a wallaby lover, and this confirms my suspicion. I look closer at it. I guess it's Old Poppy's face, except they cut off most of her forehead. What a terrible thing to take away from a kid with cute bangs.

"I didn't know wallabies were fighters," I say.

"They're *hugging*!" Aunt Blanche says. "The whiptail wallaby is the most social macropod."

"Huh," I say. "Why are there so many crystals on it?"

"For luck, joy, and to calm mental stress!" she cheers.

I sniff my gift. "Are those smells from the noxious glue?"

"Poppy, stop," Marlena scolds. "It's lovely."

That's a total lie.

"I just feel terrible Mitten Man is still missing, and I wanted to make you feel better," Aunt Blanche says.

It's amazing to me how much she fibs. She doesn't feel bad about Old Poppy's disappearance at all. She orchestrated it!

"It's perfect," Marlena says.

"Maybe you should wear it today," Aunt Blanche says.

"Maybe I should save it for a special occasion," I reply.

"Isn't every day we walk on this Earth a special occasion?" Aunt Blanche asks.

Boy, Aunt Blanche doesn't mess around. She's encroached on my territory and appears to be growing more aggressive. If I were a cat, I'd pee in her suitcase to teach her a lesson. If I still had hackles, which I wish I did, they'd be puffed up as big as a jaguar's. We're in a public battle for dominance.

"We're leaving in a couple of minutes," Don offers. "I don't think Poppy has time to change."

"Well, fine," Aunt Blanche says. "Who wants another scoop of shakshuka?"

Okay, I've won this battle. But the war with Poppy's weird-hearted aunt isn't over. If only Old Poppy were here, things would be so much better. Even though I give her a hard time, she's actually a pretty good ally. And it's nice to feel like you've got somebody on your team.

The shakshuka actually turns out to be delicious and so I do take another serving. I try to imagine what will happen during my next meal. It won't be with Heni, Rosario, or Kit, thank goodness. The four of us together never felt like a happy fit. But a certain thought keeps circling in my brain. Fifth graders and eighth graders don't normally hang out. Should I be suspicious about being sought out by them? Or should I sit back and enjoy the fact that three eighth graders can recognize my awesomeness and want to eat lunch with me and give me cookies? The answer feels obvious.

· · · · ·

It's easy to spot Sasha, Frenchie, and Xander because they are tall and kind looking and the only eighth graders I or Poppy have ever met in our whole life.

Sasha waves happily when she sees me, which feels pretty marvelous. Of course I do have to go past the friendship glob.

"Hey!" Kit says as I speed by. "We're not going to talk to you at play practice either. Deal with it."

I give her a quick nod, and try not to roll my eyes directly in her face. She's so predictable. She needs to feel like she's calling all the shots. It's so great that she and Old Poppy are finally taking a friendship break. I'm not gonna lie, it hurts a tiny bit when Heni doesn't even look at me or call out to ask about Mitten Man. But I just refocus my attention on the cookies awaiting me and the pain mostly fades.

When I slide into a chair next to Frenchie, I try not to drool as I stare at the amazing sugar cookie she's got set on a plate in front of her. It's got four perfect petals piped with bright buttery puffs of thick frosting. I think it's supposed to be a pink azalea.

"That looks so good!" I say, pointing to the cookie.

"I knew you'd love it!" she cheers, turning to Sasha. "Poppy is the perfect person for our project."

Weird to think that eighth graders consider eating cookies at lunch a project.

"Here's my cookie," Xander says. "Have you ever eaten a lambingan before? Basically, it's a sandwich cookie covered in coconut. It's my nana's recipe."

183

These three seem very excited to talk about cookies, which feels strange, because I'm only interested in eating them. Maybe this is a human/cat thing?

"And this is my s'more cookie," Sasha says, enthusiastically producing a mini-marshmallow-topped chocolate chunk treat. "I'm an expert marshmallow roaster."

"Good for you," I say, even though I don't think that's actually a skill.

"So we think we'll charge a dollar a cookie," Frenchie says. "Does that sound good to you?"

That really stops me from taking any cookies. I didn't bring any money with me. "Wait. You're charging me?" I ask. This invitation now feels like a total trick.

"Oh *gosh* no!" Xander says, shaking his head and laughing. "We're inviting you to be part of the City Kitty Helper Club. We haven't gone live yet, but here's a rough sketch of our website." He pulls out a notebook with a ton of colored pencil scribbles on it.

"And . . . when do I get to eat the totally free cookies?" I ask.

"Whenever you want!" Sasha gushes, sliding all three cookies across the table to me.

"We think you'd be a great addition to the club," Xander says.

"How often will we be eating cookies?" I ask. Because that's really the most important question.

"Principal Savage said we can sell cookies the last Friday of every month," Sasha says. "If we each make two dozen cookies, we can earn almost a hundred dollars for the Snake River Animal Shelter."

"And once the website goes up, we'll get donations that way too," Xander gushes. "We're thinking we'll share the recipes, and maybe post pictures of the animals we're helping."

"Wait," I say. "If I join the club, does that mean I've got to make cookies?"

Xander's face wrinkles in confusion. "Well, yeah."

"You can only start a club if you've got a mix of grades, remember?" Frenchie explains. "You're our fifth grader."

My own trustworthy brain nailed it, but I was too blinded by the free cookies to believe it. These eighth graders do want something from me. They're trying to force me to join a once-a-month-cookie-baking club to help support our local animal shelter, plus help out with their website. I feel pretty deceived. If there's two things I never thought I'd be in charge of when I was a cat, it's baking cookies and running a website.

"We thought you'd be more excited about this," Sasha says, sticking out her bottom lip in a pout.

That seems like a crazy thing to assume. I've never baked anything before. "Why would you think that?" I ask.

"Because you love cats," Xander says. "Didn't you win that writing contest last month with that haiku about your cat Muffin Man?"

"It's Mitten Man," I correct. "He's named after his four white paws, not some kind of quick bread!"

"Okay, okay," Frenchie says. "You don't need to yell."

I didn't realize I was yelling.

"So does this mean you don't want to join the club?" he asks.

I take a deep breath and think about it. Then I take a bite of Xander's cookie. Of course I want to join the club. This lambingan is the best thing I've bitten into this year. It's the perfect mix of soft and sweet.

"I'll join the club," I say. "I just need time to decide what kind of cookie I want to bake. And maybe ease me into the website tasks. I've got slow thumbs."

"Sure," Sasha says. "But the bake sale is next Friday, so don't take too long."

These eighth graders sure know how to pressurize a situation.

I wiggle my thumbs at them. "Got it," I say. Then I open up my lunch bag and start to eat.

"It's okay if you want to go eat with your friends now," Frenchie tells me.

Yikes. Are the eighth graders booting me from their table already? I glance back at the friendship glob. They seem really happy.

"That's okay," I say.

"Um." There's three long seconds of silence before Sasha says, "Okay."

I bite into my sandwich and for the first time really study the art in this place. The Upper Teton Middle School mascot, a brightly painted wolverine wearing a sports jersey, is painted on every wall. He's dribbling a basketball, scoring a touchdown, and swinging a baseball bat like a champion. It's all so ridiculous. A wolverine, even though it's no bigger than a medium-size dog, will attack a bear, take down a moose, and devour a mountain lion like it's a donut. A wolverine would have zero interest in spiking a volleyball.

I wonder if Old Poppy ever looked at this silly wall art and accidentally got brainwashed by it? I really hope she didn't. I hope by now she's figured out that there are many, many animals in this world actively looking to eat her. They can smell her better than she can smell herself. She's a defenseless chicken nugget out there. Even if she's careful, even if she sticks with Death Tiger, how long can she stay safe? Why hasn't she come home?

CHAPTER 14

The Nightmare Box

I can see Death Tiger's rib cage rise and fall when he breathes, and he's so tired that he doesn't snap at me anymore. I'm starting to doom spiral, which I've only done once, when I threw up on the octopus ride at Fun Land and my puke went everywhere. I still remember how helpless I felt watching my own puke get hosed out of that ride, but this is much, much worse. I feel trapped by my own decisions. I was trying to do the right thing, but now my life is a disaster. And Death Tiger's too.

"You're an excellent mouser, Mitten Man," he whispers. "Why haven't you brought back one of your famous tender rodents instead of those wild berries?"

I would really appreciate getting a suggestion for something I can actually accomplish for once. Of course I want to help find a good meal, but it seems impossible that I'll ever catch a mouse. Even if I managed to chase one down in a field and pounce on it, I doubt very much I'm capable of murdering it with my itty-bitty cat teeth. When you're a fifth grader and you encounter a mouse, it's tiny. When you're a cat, guess what, it's the size of half your leg. I know I've eaten a lot of hamburgers in my life, but this feels so different. Burgers arrive perfectly cooked inside a bun with mustard and pickles. Retrieving a mouse would be a total bloodbath.

"Here's another berry," I say, dropping it near his head. Who wouldn't want another berry?

Death Tiger licks it, but doesn't actually eat it. The sun has come and gone more than once as we try to rest and mend his leg. So far, we sleep and hunt at the same time. Death Tiger and I both think that it's too dangerous to split up. I'm still a new cat. I don't feel comfortable exploring all these fields and backyards solo. And if I wanted to go look for Raul for myself, I'm not even sure what color he is. Is Raul brown or green? Either way, he's going to merge with his environment.

I thought if we rested enough, Death Tiger would get better. But he seems so weak. Being a homeless cat is hard work. Being an injured homeless cat feels impossibly risky.

When I think about Princess Tofu now, I realize she probably met a terrible end right away. All those posters her family hung up were never going to bring her home. She needed an ally. She needed her own Death Tiger. The odds of making it alone out here are slim to zilch. I doubt whether even Kit could make it, and she comes from a family that loves to fish and bow-hunt large helpless animals. Last year her older sister helped take down a totally innocent elk.

Even though I hate looking at blood or cuts or wounds, I know I need to check Death Tiger's injury again. "Can I see your leg?" I ask.

Death Tiger moans. He drags his hind leg out from under him and rolls onto his side. Blood stains his fur from his knee to his paw, and the large gash on his leg looks almost angry. It's already infected. It's not going to heal on its own.

Do stray cats know about vets? Maybe he'll think I'm a genius when I tell him there are special animal doctors who exist to help ailing cats. "We should take you to a veterinarian," I say.

"I'm not ready to give up," Death Tiger says. "Don't you remember what Raul told us about the vet? All the animals are put in cages. Some of them die."

191

I guess that's one way to look at it. "But vets try to save you. I think they could fix something like this."

"Raul said they only help animals who have owners. Other animals get sent away and he never sees them again," Death Tiger says. "They'd never help a stray cat like me."

Did Raul work for a vet as some kind of support turtle? How does he know so much about animal clinics?

"Maybe Raul doesn't know everything," I say. I don't mean to say negative things about a turtle I've never met, but things are bad here. We should be making decisions based on what we see with our own cat eyeballs, and not follow vague guidance left behind from a missing reptile.

"You're the one who told me that Raul was the wisest animal you'd ever met," Death Tiger says. "That's the whole reason we helped him escape from his terrible home with Becky. Because you said it's wrong to keep a genius trapped in a box!"

"I'm not saying he isn't a genius, but if he saw your leg, maybe he'd feel differently," I explain. I feel extra responsible to get Death Tiger medical help. If it weren't for me wanting to wait around and watch my friendship with Heni collapse in front of my eyes, Death Tiger might not have gone off by himself and been attacked.

"I'm not going to a stranger who will put me in a cage and send me away," Death Tiger says. "Besides, without me, you won't know everything you need to know."

That might be true, but Death Tiger still needs to get to a vet.

"I haven't been totally honest with you," Death Tiger says. "I think I know where to find Raul."

I could feel super betrayed to learn this, but I don't. It's a relief to know that I'm not the only deceptive cat here.

"What?!" I ask. "Where is he? Is he okay?"

"No," Death Tiger says. "The bullies probably have him."

How come I never get good news anymore? Ever since I became a cat I feel like the world just keeps handing me all storm clouds and no rainbows. Don't I deserve at least one stinking rainbow?

"How did the bullies get him from my garage?" I ask. "How do you know this?"

"The grasshoppers," Death Tiger says. "While I've been resting they've been pestering me nonstop. I try not to listen, but they say Raul is being tortured and there's no way I can save him."

Another storm cloud! Basically, my life has become a bad-news hurricane. No wonder Death Tiger hates listening to the grasshoppers.

"Do you know where the bullies live?" I ask. I don't really want to go looking for intimidating jerks, but I might have to do just that.

"They've got him at the spider building."

The what?! Is he being serious?! "The spider building?" I say. "Where's that?"

Death Tiger licks between the toe pads of his dirtiest paw. How can he be calm when his good friend is being tortured in a SPIDER BUILDING? "The building where they make the sticky spider traps. The one with the vicious dog."

Vicious dog?! How is it possible that everything keeps getting worse?

"This is a lot of stuff to withhold from me," I say. "Why didn't you tell me sooner?"

"You've been acting so weird," Death Tiger says.

That's actually a fair assessment.

"Well, at least you've told me everything now," I say. "Right?"

"There's one more thing," Death Tiger whispers. "They keep Raul in a Nightmare Box."

Wow. How did my life turn into an actual horror movie? There's no way I can doom spiral, because I am already at the lowest point imaginable. Seriously. I've reached the trapdoor, in the basement, beneath a tunnel, below an ocean, under the earth's lower mantle, and it's full of the most awful doom knowledge that a person-turned-cat could ever learn. If what the grasshoppers chirp is true, which it probably is, I live in a neighborhood that has a spider building in it with a Nightmare Box, guarded by a vicious dog, and I'm most likely going to have to go there by myself to rescue a turtle named Raul.

"You'd think the grasshoppers would do something to help somebody instead of just coming up with terrifying rhymes," I say. I'm sort of hoping, even though it's unlikely, that maybe the grasshoppers will band together and assist me in the rescue. They could swarm somebody or spit brown goo on them or something.

"Grasshoppers have been on this earth as long as dinosaurs and they've only caused destruction."

"You're right. I forgot they were as old as dinosaurs," I say. "My third grade teacher told me that."

As I say those words, I realize what I've done.

"Huh?" Death Tiger asks. "What's third grade?"

It's too much pressure. Why bother lying at this point? If Death Tiger is admitting he wasn't totally honest with me, I need to admit that I haven't been totally honest with him either. This truth wants out.

"Okay. Fine. I can't do this anymore. What I'm going to tell you next is the absolute truth," I say. I take one deep breath. Then another. "I am not Mitten Man."

Death Tiger stares at me with shocked, unblinking eyes.

"Yes. I am actually a fifth-grade girl," I continue. "My name is Poppy McBean. My cat, Mitten Man, your friend, and I switched places a few days ago. This collar probably had something to do with it. At first, we tried to switch back. But then Mitten Man really liked being a person and trying new foods. And he also promised me he'd help me out with some problems I was having at school—which he absolutely didn't! He actually made my human life much worse. And also, we can't figure out how to switch back. So I'm not Mitten Man, I'm Poppy, which is why I'm so terrible at catching mice and climbing tall stuff. I'm so, so sorry I lied to you. But now that I'm here with you in this situation, I really want to help you save Raul."

Death Tiger doesn't gasp at my confession, or strike me in anger. In fact, he just sighs.

"So it's that werewolf story all over again," Death Tiger says.

"No," I say. "How did you get a werewolf out of my confession?"

Death Tiger rolls his sunken eyes at me. "How is this any different than the time that Labrador slobbered on you during a full moon and you told me you'd been turned into a werewolf? You're full of crazy ideas and drama. You're the one who lured Raul out of his fenced-in area. You're the reason he's being tortured. He got stolen from your garage. Face it, Mitten Man, you make bad things happen."

My cat does not make bad things happen and neither do I! I feel really insulted. But it's hard to stay mad at a seriously wounded cat. Death Tiger needs my help, even if he thinks I'm a bad-luck curse, which I am not.

"It's a waste of time to fight," I say. When I look at him, when I make myself really consider that injury, I realize he won't be able to help me rescue Raul. I think I've known that from the start.

"Let me sleep," Death Tiger says, dragging himself underneath a bush. "Rest will fix me, that's what you said."

I shake my head. "You need more than rest at this point. Your wound is infected. You need antibiotics."

"NO," Death Tiger says. "I'm staying here."

I don't know how to convince a stubborn cat to do something he doesn't want to do. But maybe if I can't, somebody else can. "So how close is this spider building?"

Death Tiger aims a paw in a very specific direction. "Just one hayfield away."

I know what I need to do. I need to enter that place, rescue Raul, and then bring him back here. If he really is a genius, if he sees that Death Tiger's leg is infected, he'll tell him he needs to go to the vet. And since Raul is responsible for Death Tiger's distrust of veterinarians in the first place, his advice will fix everything. I think this fifth-grade logic works.

I take a deep breath and ask myself the most important question of my life: *Do I smell weasels?* No. And I don't know how long this weedy area will stay weasel-free, so I need to act fast.

"I'm going to rescue Raul," I say. "Do you have any advice before I go?"

"Watch out for the bullies, watch out for the dog, and try to enter the building through the loading doors before they close them for the day."

"I will try to do all of those things," I say. "And don't worry, I'm not going to say goodbye, because I'm going to be back soon."

"You've been a good friend," Death Tiger says, his voice tinged with a sadness so deep that it lifts up my neck fur. "I'll miss you."

"Stop it, Death Tiger! I'm not dying and neither are you," I say. "Not today!"

"I'd like to believe that," Death Tiger says.

As I leave my new friend and enter a clover patch, I hear the grasshoppers burst into song.

"Bullies are too hard to fight.

Turn around. You know we're right."

CHAPTER 15
Pizza Points

One big problem with middle school is you can't escape unlikable kids, because the hallway system feeds you into their paths against your will. As I wander back to class after lunch, I spot Deezil, a real mood-wrecker, coming straight toward me. He's got his phone out and is showing people pictures. I try not to look, but he jams it right in my face.

"Pancake on my turtle!" he yells.

I duck under his arm and keep heading to class. Wait. Was that Raul underneath a giant pancake? What's wrong with Deezil? How does a fifth grader wind up becoming such a pitiful bully? I add "Raul under a pancake" to my stack of problems I need to solve soon. But finding Old Poppy trumps everything else right now. At least my turtle friend is getting fed well. That pancake looked super fluffy and delicious.

When I get to the classroom I notice two things: All the solar eclipse art assignments are pinned to the wall (except mine) and the white board has streamers taped to it. There's also balloons attached to the marker shelf. The song "Here We Have Idaho" starts playing on a loop from a small speaker on Ms. Gish's desk. What's going on? Am I about to experience my first human dance party? I know I should get my solar eclipse art out of my backpack. That's the responsible thing to do. But Ms. Gish has a roll of tape out and is furiously securing the speaker wires to the floor. Is this really the best time to bug her and beg her not to dock me points? Won't there be a better time in the future, when I actually feel like doing it? And won't this time happen when my teacher isn't biting tape into pieces? And won't this time also happen when awesome music beats aren't bouncing off the walls making my whole body want to dance? I gotta do some stretches.

"The pizza party gets decided today," a boy cheers.

I've never seen this kid before. I'm bending down to touch my toes, and even upside down I can see that he's tall and has long blond hair and purple glasses. Then he sits in my desk and I immediately know who he is. I flip back to standing.

"Where's all my stuff?" he asks.

Super weird this kid missed half the day and then came to school for the pizza party dance. There should be a rule against doing that. "You must be sick Max," I say.

"I'm just Max," he says. "I got better."

"Well, I'm Poppy and I have your desk now."

"You don't need to tell me that. I know who you are. We're Hot Seat partners," Max says.

"Excuse me?" I say. The idea of having a hot seat actually sounds fun. "Where is this magical heater seat located?"

"Um, the vocab game. Hot Seat. Did they give you a new partner while I was gone?" Max asks.

"Not sure," I say. "Pleasure meeting you, Hot Seat Max."

I'm not going to lie, it bothers me when Heni, Rosario, and Kit enter the room and they all refuse to look at me. When I was a cat, I didn't mind being a loner. In fact, I preferred it. Being in a classroom abuzz with activity, though, I don't exactly miss Old Poppy's friends, but I do feel left out. And I feel extra left out by Heni.

The starting bell goes off, and even though I know it's going to happen, I can't help but scream. People are used to it now though. Nobody even looks at me.

"As you can tell by our decorations," Ms. Gish is saying, "today is our final day for pizza points. Whatever table ends up with the most points wins the pizza party."

"Woohoo!" I yell, jumping to my feet. I'm surprised other kids aren't doing the same. Free pizza? If there's one thing I know about fifth grade, it's that free pizza doesn't happen every day.

"But before we get to that, I have one request and one piece of bad news."

I gasp and clutch my heart. I hope it's not related to the pizza party I just learned about. The Idaho music stops playing.

"First, the request. My daughter's kindergarten class is mastering scissor work this week. And I'm looking for volunteers to donate your solar eclipse art projects so her class can practice cutting circles. Are any students willing to donate their amazing projects for a good cause?"

Everybody except for three people raises their hand: Kit, Rosario, and me. Great. I do not want to be in any sort of group with a toxic masterpiece and a flavorless follower, even if it's an informal anti-art-destroying trio, so I shoot my hand up so fast I almost launch out of my desk. Maybe now Ms. Gish won't notice I'm turning in the project so late.

"Great! I'll donate those after we use them at the solar eclipse this week."

Sick Max raises his hand before she can tell us the bad news. "Did you know that the speed of the moon as it crosses the sun is 1,398 miles per hour?"

A bunch of kids *ooh* at this. I guess I understand why Heni likes Sick Max so much. His brain crunches huge outer-space numbers. It's impressive.

"Thank you, Max," Ms. Gish says. "Now for the bad news: Ms. Dance won't be starting play rehearsals yet. She's out sick."

"I heard she got bit by a toxic spider," Kit says.

I flip around. Can that be true?

"It's true," Ms. Gish says. "Ms. Dance got bit by a hobo spider. She's doing okay, but she's had a severe reaction. She'll be out the rest of the week. The important thing is she'll be okay."

I clutch my heart and gasp again. That's a long time to ask me to forgo singing and dancing like a clown—the only reason I like being a person.

"I hate spiders so much," Heni says. "They're hairy and scary."

Ms. Gish lets out a big sigh and sits down on the edge of her desk. "Let's not hate on spiders. They're important contributors to the ecosystem. Without them, our food supply would be overrun by pests."

The world feels so complicated. If we want to have food, we also need to exist alongside toxic spiders. What a tragedy. Especially for Ms. Dance.

"Now let's assemble our Geography Tables," Ms. Gish says.

Everybody around me starts to squish desks together, so I try to do the same thing.

"You're *not* at my table," Kit barks at me. "Back it up."

I maneuver my desk to another group. "What are you doing?" Rosario asks. "This isn't your table. You don't belong here."

"My cat's missing, Rosario," I say. "You should be nicer to me."

I pick up my desk and do a full rotation. Rosario gives me a very disgusted look, like I'm made out of poison or something. Thankfully, just then Sick Max waves at me, so I waddle over and set my desk next to his. Luckily, Heni is also in my group, along with a girl with bright red hair, which I think might actually be a wig, so I tug on it.

"Ouch," she says.

"I was trying to get a bug out," I lie.

"Okay," Ms. Gish says. "Let's turn on our Idaho brains. Today we're going to ask questions about our rivers, mountains, and state symbols. Red Team, you're first."

Kit bounces up to the front of the class. "So I'm going to call on the Green Team," she says, disguising her bossy voice to sound sweet.

"Don't forget to say how much the question is worth," Ms. Gish says.

"This is for two points," Kit says. "What's the biggest lake in Idaho?"

Madison shoots her hand up right away, confirming my theory about fifth graders that those who wear sequins move faster than those who don't.

"Lake Pend Oreille," Madison says.

"Correct," Ms. Gish says.

Kit uses a black marker to draw two lines next to the Green Team. Then Madison hops up and stands up in front of the class.

"I pick the Yellow Team," she says. "For two points."

Max and Heni and the redheaded girl seem very excited, and that's when I realize I'm on the Yellow Team.

"What's the tallest mountain in Idaho?" Madison asks.

I rocket to my feet. "Mount Borah! It's in the Lost River Range! In Salmon-Challis National Forest! Don't try to climb it unless you bring an ice axe. Or else you'll never make it past Chicken Out Ridge!" Then I wiggle my butt, flap my elbows, and do a winner dance. "Clucka clucka!"

Who knew a boring conversation with Don could pay off for me one day? I feel like I should get at least six points for knowing such important mountain information. My team stares at me in complete surprise as I continue my strut and cluck around my desk.

Madison marks two black lines for our team and skips back to her seat. I zoom full speed to take my spot at the front of the classroom. I feel so powerful standing next to the white board, holding a black marker. It's the first time in my life I've ever held a marker! I take the cap off and sniff it.

"Don't smell Sharpies," Ms. Gish says firmly. "And don't write with it on the board either. Use the dry-erase ones." Max hands me a different marker. I feel like I'm learning the secrets of the universe.

"I'm going to call on the Purple Team," I say.

"Do you mean the Blue Team?" Ms. Gish asks. "We don't have a Purple Team."

"I mean the Blue Team," I say.

What a tragedy that the class doesn't have a purple team. It's such a fantastic color.

There's a knock on the door, which means Ms. Gish leaves me standing all by myself at the front of the classroom. It feels like I'm the teacher. I watch as she steps into the hall-way and closes the door.

"How many points?" a tiny voice asks.

I don't even hesitate on the number. "Fifty thousand points."

Everybody gasps. I've really made this game exciting. I feel electric and alive, like I was built for this moment. I try hard to think about something I know about Idaho. Poppy has mentioned a few moderately interesting things about this state over the years. I tap my head. And it comes to me. "Okay. What is the state fruit of Idaho?"

So many hands shoot up it surprises me. These kids are bigger fruit nerds than I realized.

"Mason," I say. Because I haven't bothered to learn many kids' names, and he helped me move my desk to the sunny spot.

"The huckleberry!" Mason says. "I just won fifty-thousand points!"

"Truth," I say.

I hear a bunch of grumbling as I start drawing little black lines on the white board next to the Blue Team. I've never drawn 50,000 black lines before, but it seems like this will take a few minutes.

"What happened?" Ms. Gish asks, coming back in.

"We won the pizza party!" Mason cheers.

I keep drawing lines.

"Poppy, why are you drawing so many lines?" Ms. Gish asks.

"They won fifty-thousand points," I explain.

"Nobody won fifty-thousand points. Nothing is worth that much in this game," Ms. Gish says.

I keep drawing lines. I'm only at thirty-two.

"Poppy. Mason. In the hallway," Ms. Gish says. "Everybody else read to yourself until I get back."

Mason seems stunned to be called to the hallway, but nothing surprises me anymore about fifth grade. This place has a lot of tricky corners.

Ms. Gish quietly closes the classroom door. The hallway feels very long and echoey when it's mostly empty.

"What happened in there?" Ms. Gish asks.

"I knew Idaho's state fruit and won fifty thousand points," Mason explains.

"That's what happened," I agree.

"Did you two plan to steal the pizza party?" Ms. Gish asks.

Mason looks so upset by this question, but I understand where Ms. Gish is coming from. He does look very much like an accomplice.

"NO!" Mason gushes. "I would *never* do that!"

"Okay, you can go back in the classroom," Ms. Gish says, and I turn to leave. "I was talking to Mason."

I turn back around.

"This isn't like you, Poppy. Is there something you want to talk about?" she asks.

She's so kind that I feel a little bit bad about wrecking her pizza game. I didn't mean to torpedo it. I just wanted to dial up the drama, amp up the fun.

"I guess things are really terrible at home," I explain. "My hippie aunt from Fresno came to visit and took over my room and sent my beloved cat into the wilderness and bought me a toxic shirt my parents want me to wear even though I'm worried about the plasticizers in it."

"Wow," Ms. Gish says. "That does sound tough."

"It is. Because it's really hard to find a cat after it runs away and you don't know where to look. Also, I have to sleep in the office now and the pullout couch hurts my back and I'm pretty sure there are spiders in the closet. And now I'm afraid they might be toxic, because of what happened to Ms. Dance."

"This is all a lot," she says. "I can talk to your parents about the spiders."

"Plus I've gotten locked out of my own house a couple of times," I say. "Other people's crimes keep both my parents pretty busy these days." I keep searching my brain. "And Kit, Heni, and Rosario dumped me and don't want to be friends anymore because I got a better part than they did in the school play. I mean, they basically hate me because I've got fresh moves." Then I dance a little bit for her.

"That's certainly something I can address," she says with a voice so gentle I feel hugged by it. "Is that everything?"

I shake my head. This is a good moment to ask for forgiveness. "I forgot to turn in my solar eclipse art project and even though I'm donating it to your kid's cutting crew, it's currently very crumpled and still inside my backpack and I'm worried I won't get any points if I turn it in, because you have a brutal late homework policy. Also, I spilled milk on it and now it's crunchy."

It feels like Ms. Gish is forcing herself not to react with her face to what I'm saying. "Go get your assignment and I'll hang it up right now. I left you a spot next to Heni."

"Did you do that on your own or did Heni ask you to do that?" I ask. My heartbeat races.

"She asked."

"*When?*" Maybe she didn't really dump me all the way.

"A couple of days ago," Ms. Gish says.

"Oh." My joy collapses into sad mush. "Heni ended our friendship yesterday, so that timeline doesn't change anything."

Ms. Gish gives me a huge, reassuring smile. "Let's go back to class and give the Blue Team two points and play for the Pizza Party again. And you can turn in your art project. Full credit. We'll hang it next to Heni's."

"Most of this sounds great," I say. "Except it's gonna be a huge bummer for Mason."

"I think he'll understand," Ms. Gish says.

As we go back into the classroom, she puts her hand on my shoulder. "You're doing great, Poppy," she says. "Just, when a bad thing happens, try your best not to make it worse."

Huh. That's really gonna stick in my brain.

I wonder. Is that what I've been doing my whole life? I sit at my desk and hear the clock tick. Maybe I'm not as helpless as I think I am when it comes to all my life's disasters.

Most importantly, maybe I do know where to look for a lost cat.

CHAPTER 16

Hairball Hider

According to Death Tiger, the spider building is one hay-field away. I stop to catch my breath and go over the rescue plan. I think I have it all clear in my head. And if I hear a strange sound or catch a weird smell, I plan to abandon whatever I'm doing and run up a tall tree.

I'm kind of shocked to find myself here. Not even Kit would attempt something so risky. Which means that I am now the boldest person I know. Except I'm a cat.

And it's go time!

Wait. For some reason in this moment I can't stop myself from urgently licking my belly fur. I'm actually making a bald spot. Whoa. What a strange and powerful tongue. I speed up my licks. After everything Mitten Man has put me through, he deserves a million bald spots. Okay. It's go time for real. RUN!

I reach a tall chain-link fence and stop. A big corrugated metal building sits on the other side of it. Luckily, both delivery doors are open. One has a giant pickup truck backed into it. Can I really make it over this thing? Once, Heni tried to climb over a fence near the school and her jeans got caught and I had to rip her down, and her underwear showed through the hole in her pants all the way home. Nobody in her family could even mend them. She had to throw them out. I don't want history to repeat itself.

What would Death Tiger do? Of course. He'd find the easy way. There's a perfect place to race underneath, so I squeeze through it. On the other side of the fence I was scared. On this side I'm terrified. There are signs everywhere warning about a variety of dangerous things. Dogs. Private Property. Adhesives. One sign has a skull and crossbones on it that says NOTHING INSIDE IS WORTH DYING FOR. I begin to blaze down this dirt road faster than Dominique Sanchez, the fastest runner at my school, who moves so quickly when she races track that she's just a wavy-haired blur in blue shorts. Then I hear the barks.

When I was Old Poppy I didn't really like dogs, but they were okay. They always tried to sniff my crotch and I couldn't stand how they smelled wet. But I'd never had a terrible or terrifying experience with one. Until now. Is this how everything will end for me? Eaten by a dog while trespassing on a spider compound trying to rescue a turtle from his torturers while thinking about my middle-school track star? As a cat?

But the dog's teeth never tear into me. I hear a clink and a clank sound over and over, and even though it might be stupid, I stop and look over my shoulder. Oh, phew! That maniac dog can't get me. He's chained up. The sound of a dog not devouring you is a truly great thing to hear. But this bliss gets interrupted when I hear the sound of a truly terrible thing to hear. It's the sound of a voice I cannot stand. It's the sound of Deezil Wolfinger.

My first thought is: *How could Deezil Wolfinger be Raul's torturer?*

My next thought is: *Of course Deezil Wolfinger is Raul's torturer.* It makes total sense that Deezil is somehow caught up in turtle torture and has commanded his angry dog to

demolish me. Deezil's not just your typical bully. He's a ty-
rant. As long as that kid has arms, he'll push other people
(and their cats) around.

"Get her, Garf!" Deezil says. "Destroy that cat."

And with that he sets Garf loose.

I take off running so fast I forget to close my mouth
and swallow a bug. That dog reaches me just as I get to
the tree on the side of the building and spring as high as
I've ever sprung. The dog leaps too, but all he catches is air.
Using my claws, I stick to the tree's side like Velcro. Yes!
Take that, Garf! And Deezil! And Kit! And anybody who
ever doubted me!

What would Heni say if she could see me now? I know
she's mad at me, but if she could see the risks I'm taking to
save a helpless turtle, maybe some of her anger would melt
away.

I'm going to be so different when I'm Poppy again. I'll
give Heni a million apologies and explanations. And if she
believes me *and* forgives me, maybe our friendship will
somehow be better. Sometimes when something breaks, it

re-forms stronger; my science teacher told our class that about bonds. I think he was talking about atoms, but aren't Heni and I made out of atoms? Shouldn't that science rule work for us too?

After I catch my breath I realize that I can't stay pasted to a tree like this. Deezil will just come knock me down.

Luckily, I'm right next to the building now. Progress! Then I see the open window. It's far, but if I focus, how far can I really jump? I make a mental measurement of where I need to go. When I picture the leap in my head, I don't make it. I replace myself with Dominique. She doesn't make it either. That's a bad sign.

I picture Heni and I imagine that I'm leaping high over the fence with her again. I lock my eyes on the window. That's my goal. I can make it. I leap from the tree and begin to plummet like a stone. I feel like a failure as I sail to the ground, watching the window get further away. But this all changes the moment I hit that trash can lid with a fierce bounce up, high enough to skitter in through the open window, dive onto a four-wheeler, and catapult myself into a speedboat. I did it! Which is something I need to always remember. Don't ever give up on anything in life, even when you think you're dog food, because a random trash can lid might bounce you where you need to go.

Once I catch my breath, I realize that the speedboat is the perfect place to be. I can see everything and still remain hidden. I peek out of the boat as a much taller torturer enters the warehouse with Garf at his side, barking like crazy. He can smell me, I know it. I guess I did know that Deezil had a brother, Whip, but because I'm an optimist I didn't expect him to be a jumbo bully.

"Come on, Garf," Whip says. "Back on the chain."

Garf keeps barking at me. But luckily these are some lazy bullies. "I don't see anything," he says, and turns and leaves, pulling the tall garage door down and locking it after he exits.

And now it's time to find Raul. At this rate, I'll be able to make it back to Death Tiger when it's still daylight. Aren't weasels active only at night? After straining my small cat brain with worry, and doom spiraling, everything is going to be fine. Death Tiger might be at the vet before sundown.

Uh-oh. Did the bullies shut the window? They did. Without it I don't have an exit strategy. Until this moment, I've never needed an exit strategy. I just followed my school's bell schedule and opened and closed doors when the need arose. I look around the giant cement space packed with boxes and equipment. How will it be possible to locate something the size of a turtle in a place this big? And escape from a doorless, windowless building? And make it back to my wounded friend?

I carefully leap out of the speedboat and begin pouncing on boxes. All I see are packaged spider traps, which appear to be thin pieces of cardboard covered in glue, wrapped in plastic. I read one of the packages: INDOOR SPIDER TRAPS. PRE-BAITED. NO POISON. There's a picture of a terrifyingly big spider stuck to a trap. Yikes. I hope I never encounter anything this scary.

I need to think like a cat. Maybe I can smell a turtle more easily than I can spot one. I try breathing deeply. It's bonkers to me that my nose can pick up so many different scents: cardboard, tension brakes, push broom, gasoline, tool chests. *Sniff. Sniff.* Bingo! I smell a reptile. I hurry over to a laundry basket and peer inside. Raul, who's the size of a small dinner plate, aims both of his bright orange eyes at me. The green and turquoise pattern spread across his shell looks like the most beautiful mosaic I've ever seen. I sort of understand why a person would steal Raul. He looks like a living piece of fine art.

"Raul!" I say. "I'm here to rescue you!"

Raul retracts his head into his brilliant shell with a snap.

"Beat it!" Raul's response is muffled but full of rage.

"But I'm here to help you," I explain. Can he even hear me when his head is in the shell? Maybe if I gently pet him, I can coax him out. I reach my paw out and softly rub the top of his shell. "Raul, I have something important to tell you."

Out of nowhere, I'm struck by a terrible feeling. It's something that I've never felt before. There's something inside of me that wants out. I start to gag—like, full-body gagging, everything from my nose to my dewclaw getting involved. "Ack! Hack! Gack!" My insides twist like a washing machine. "Ick! Ugh! Blech!" Finally I hurl a vomit wad onto the cement floor. It splats right next to the basket.

"You are a gross excuse for a rescuer," Raul says.

"Not fair, Raul," I say. "Hairballs happen." I'm truly surprised by the power of that hairball. It shot out of me like a cannon ball! I guess I did over-lick my belly fur. I will *not* make that mistake again. I feel like my stomach found an escape route out my mouth.

"First, you betray me. Then you spit furballs at me." He sticks out his head and looks up at me. "You are the worst friend ever!"

"Don't re-shell yourself," I plead. "Let me explain!"

How do you sincerely apologize to a turtle you've never met for a bunch of stuff you never did?

"You told me the guard bat would keep me safe!" Raul snaps.

"At the time I believed that bat to be very fierce," I say, guessing wildly. "I'm sorry it didn't work out."

"And you promised I'd get to Carl's farm. Instead, I was stolen by cruel maniacs. They torture me. They pull things out of their Nightmare Box, sometimes heavy things, like a wrench or a ceramic mug. Sometimes they are smelly things like old cheese or a moldy tortilla. Sometimes they are weird things like a small hat or a plastic pickle. They use those things to make my life the absolute worst. One day, they stacked seven rubber ducks on top of me. Once, they built a tower out of toilet paper. And then they taunt me. They yell, 'Stuff on my turtle!' And flash a light at me."

"They're monsters," I say. But I'm starting to wonder if this might be something other than a torture situation. Are Whip and Deezil taking Raul's picture? Is that what the flash means? Maybe they're posting the photos online or sending them to their friends. How do I explain the internet and social media to a turtle who doesn't trust me?

"And if that doesn't take the cake, they've also started painting me," Raul says.

This actually sounds very bad. Then I notice not one, but two purple dots spray-painted onto him.

"Raul, those dots they've painted on you are toxic. We need to get you out of that basket and to a safe place."

"No more dirty garages," he says. "Carl's farm or bust."

"Deal," I say. I'll probably need to deliver Raul to the vet too, for some nonirritating paint removal. Afterward, finding Carl's farm, whoever he is, can't be any harder than finding a lost turtle. "I'll need to flip you to get you out of there," I say, distracting him with practicalities. "Gently on three."

I put all my weight onto the edge of the plastic basket, toppling it onto its side. Raul spills out onto the cement floor.

"Does it hurt where they painted you?" I ask.

"Not really," Raul says. "But I want it off."

"Smart," I say. "Last year, in fourth-grade science, we watched a herpetologist's video about turtle facts. And one thing they told us is that turtle and tortoise painting is a huge problem. When people paint their shells, chemicals get in their blood. It also causes breathing problems and can block them from getting important vitamins from the sun."

"Well, that doesn't make me feel any better," Raul says. "What's fourth grade?"

"Um, I'll explain that later," I say.

"All I want is a home," Raul says. "A place where I can feel safe and happy."

"I get it. If you come with me," I'm so sincere when I say this, even my fur softens, "I promise this time I won't let you down."

When I think about how hard it's going to be for me to get this turtle out of this spider building and deliver him to Carl's farm, I realize I *am* going to need Big Poppy's help after all. Rage bubbles up inside of me when I think about her. After I saw her do what she did to Heni, how can I ever trust her again?

"Let's make our way to the shipping doors. When Whip opens them in the morning, we'll sneak out. Then we'll make our way to the fence," I say.

"That plan will get us killed!" Raul says.

I take a minute to think about it. Between Garf and Whip and Deezil and everything else dangerous out there, Raul and I do face total obliteration. How can we just walk out of here? Especially when one of us is a turtle?

I glance around the spider building. There are boxes of all sizes. Aha! I know what we can do. Using all my strength, I run and knock into a tall stack of empty boxes ready for shipment, scattering them across the floor. Then I look for one that a turtle will fit inside. It's so light, I bat it with my paws to steer it back to Raul.

"This is a much better idea," I say.

Raul frowns at me. "You can't carry a box out of here. You're a cat."

I turn the box upside down and place it over Raul. "It's the perfect disguise," I say. "Whip will be busy gathering the knocked-over boxes for the morning delivery truck. And we'll sneak off. You can creep away at your own speed un-detected. Once you get to the grass, lose the box and blend in with the greenery."

Raul lifts his head up from under the box. "It's actually cozy in here."

I try to smile, but my lips don't really do that in this body. So I just curl up next to boxed Raul and wait for day to come.

As much as I try not to think about Heni, she keeps walking around in my brain. Memories of her flash like movies as I try to fall asleep. I miss her.

I hold my breath and try really hard not to feel anything. But it doesn't work. Heni trips through my mind and my heart. Real friends are sticky like that. Even when you put them down, they pop back up.

CHAPTER 17

Bummer Glue

I open the door to my house and discover Aunt Blanche up-side down in a headstand in the middle of the living room. She looks like a bat.

"Namaste," she says with a giant exhale.

"Are you the only person here?" I ask. I try not to sound massively bitter and disappointed, but that's exactly how my question lands.

Aunt Blanche kicks herself over, spilling her hair over her face. "Sometimes when I'm upset, I recenter myself by sniffing calming floral scents. How do you feel about bergamot?"

Who does this? Who comes to your house, throws your cat into the wilderness, weirdly inverts herself instead of fixing after-school snacks, and suggests smelling citrus fruit to *relax?*

"I think I just wanna smell the spare room," I say. It's here I know I can figure out a plan. I've got two arms. I have access to seven pairs of shoes and at least nine forks. My brain is the size of a cantaloupe. Seriously, it should weigh three pounds. Of course I'll take a break from masterminding the rescue operation and eat dinner, where I'll exchange polite chitchat with Don and Marlena and acknowledge Aunt Blanche. But when night falls I'm outta here. Nothing will stop me from finding poor, vulnerable Old Poppy. I've got a mission. I'm unstoppable.

• • • • •

The light to my room flips on and Aunt Blanche rushes inside basically before I'm even conscious. The sudden brightness feels like a slap. Uh-oh. It's morning. What a terrible realization. After eating a troughful of vegan lasagna, I guess I slept like a rock. And forgot to wake up and concoct a viable plan to locate and/or rescue Old Poppy. Have I always been so distractable when I sleep?

"I know you're upset with me, but today I'm going to help you. Pretend like I was never here!"

My light flips off, the door closes, and Aunt Blanche vanishes. What a terrible thing to do to a sleeping person filled with regret. Now I'm awake *and* annoyed *and* disappointed.

One minute later, my light flips on again. This time, both my parents stand over me, looking stern.

"We can't eat breakfast with you today, because we need to meet with your principal," Marlena says, anger jumping out of her eyeballs and landing on me.

"Can't she meet you in the afternoon?" I ask.

"No," Don says with a very displeased tone. "I've got jury duty. They don't let you skip that even if your fifth grader is wreaking havoc."

I sit straight up. Am I in trouble? What did I do?

"I don't know why the principal wants to talk to you," I say. But really, I'm pretty sure it's about all the terrible stuff I told Ms. Gish.

"Well, that makes three of us," Marlena says. "Climbing that tree during the fire drill was a serious violation of your school's citizenship expectations. Maybe she wants to talk about that."

"Maybe," I say.

"Aunt Blanche will get you breakfast and help you get on the bus," Don says. "And tonight we're going to have a serious family meeting."

Watching Poppy's parents pack up their stuff and storm out of the house to meet with the principal feels unpleasant. So does eating cold crunchy cereal across from Aunt Blanche. And I have to admit, I've done a few things wrong. I mean, it's crazy to expect that I'd be a perfect fifth grader. So few kids are. Maybe I should've listened more to Poppy. Maybe things wouldn't be as bad as they are right now if she were sitting at my feet, offering fifth-grade guidance. I need to get her back in my life pronto. No more excuses. No more delays. Tonight can't come soon enough.

"You look very unhappy," Aunt Blanche says, staring at me.

"Probably because my life is going very terribly at the moment," I tell her.

"You don't seem to be enjoying that cereal," she says, reaching across the table and plucking my bowl away. "Why don't you eat whatever you want, and I won't tell your parents."

I give her a doubtful look. It's hard to trust a serial liar.

"I told you, I'm making things right with you. Today is your day. Whatever you want, I'll do my best to make it happen," she says.

What else have I got to lose? I walk over to the pantry and pull out the thing I'm craving. Salmon kibble. I don't even bother pouring it into a bowl. I just grab a handful out of the box and chomp on it.

"I thought that was for cats," Aunt Blanche says.

I shrug. "It tastes good to me."

She reaches her own hand in the box and taps the box's ingredient list. "Not bad. My diet needs more flax seeds," she says, grabbing a few pieces.

Is this where I want to be? Eating cat food with Poppy's hippie-treacherous aunt? Wearing pants? Sigh. I miss my old life. I'm tired of going to school and pretending to learn. Factoring isn't a practical skill for me. Neither is knowing when to use a semicolon. Yes, I want to be a dancing clown, but that's all I want to be. No more cursive writing or Idaho history. No more spider-shoed bullies. No more imaginary school fires. No more friendship glob. Even the good stuff, like my new cookie friends, comes with snags. In this moment, I've never wanted anything more desperately than to be who I am meant to be: Mitten Man. As soon as I find Old Poppy, I will figure out a way for us to switch back.

"Now, you do you today, as I told you," Aunt Blanche says. "But I do just want to point out that the bus will be here in ten minutes and you're still wearing your pajamas."

I look down at my pajamas. I don't feel like changing. Why do I always have to be putting on different clothes? It's such a waste of time. Back when I had fur all I had to do was lick it. *Ta-da*. No need to reinvent the wheel every day.

"I'm just gonna wear this," I say.

Aunt Blanche's eyes grow big with concern. But it's hard for me to believe she's really all that worried about me.

"Your parents will be furious if I let you wear hot-pink jellyfish jammies and slippers to school," she says, clearly regretting this whole "my day" thing.

An idea pops into my head. Why am I waiting for nightfall to solve my problems?

"Maybe I don't need to go to school today," I say.

"You want to stay home and read magazines with me?" she asks.

This lady doesn't get me at all. "No, I want to go and look for my poor, lost cat."

Aunt Blanche blinks a bunch.

"I'm leaving tomorrow anyway," she says. "Helping you find your plucky friend feels like the least I could do."

I'm no dummy. This sandalwood-scented person could change her mind in an instant. I throw on some sneakers and race to her car.

For safety reasons, I ride in the back seat and offer my driving suggestions from there. To find Old Poppy, I need to think like Old Poppy. She ran off with Death Tiger. And she hasn't come back. How are those two even getting along? Should I be looking for two cats or one? Is there anything that they'd bond over? That's when it hits me: I need to be looking for two cats and a turtle!

For as long as I've known her, Poppy McBean has been determined to rescue lost animals. I mean, other than finding me at the shelter, she's never been successful, but it's something she's talked about since the first time she saw a lost pet sign taped to a lamppost in first grade. Of course she'd try to rescue Raul, especially because Death Tiger has been such a fan of that turtle. I bet those two are trying to rescue him from underneath that pancake as we speak. Which means I need to get to Deezil's house. Luckily, he'll be at school, so I'll probably be able to snoop around and find everybody pretty easily. If Aunt Blanche is willing to dig through people's trash for bottles and throw their cats into the wilderness for joy, maybe she'll help me break into a house for a rescue mission too.

"Which way now?" Aunt Blanche asks me.

"Left," I say. Whenever I don't know which way to turn I always go left. That's called trusting your gut. And I was born with a top-notch one. "I need to go to Deezil Wolfinger's house. Can we look up where he lives on your phone?"

I know I'm right. Old Poppy loves to talk about her dreams with me. Night after night, snuggled beside me, she's always gone on and on about wanting to rescue helpless little beings. She even saves disgusting slimy sidewalk worms. Poppy has a heart as squishy as a marshmallow and as big as a moon. Would Old Poppy try to fix something so unfixable as finding a lost turtle she's never met as a species she's never been? Totally.

"Is it possible Deezil Wolfinger's parents own a spider trap–packaging business located on Willow Creek Lane?" Aunt Blanche is peering at her phone.

"Very possible," I say. "We need to get to that spider traps place now!"

We turn left again.

"Your bedroom/office does have some issues in that department," Aunt Blanche says. "But rather than traps, allow me to say, *pirate spider*. It's a spider that enjoys eating other spiders. When I'm trying to solve a problem, I try to think holistically. And I don't think traps are a humane solution to an arachnid or mammalian problem."

Pirate spiders have massive fangs. No way the McBean fam would invite one into their house. Aunt Blanche does not solve problems like a normal person. I admire that.

"I don't need spider traps. I think Mitten Man might be there," I explain. "And maybe a turtle I lost."

The closer we get, the more familiar everything feels: a wide canal, alfalfa fields, long gravel driveway, and the giant metal workshop. This is the place.

"They don't look open," Aunt Blanche says.

"Just drive up to the doors," I say.

I watch as a familiar shape walks toward us. Whip, the big bully. He lets his dog off the chain anytime we're near. But now that we're roughly the same size, I don't feel scared of him at all. I'm an adorable fifth grader wearing delightful jellyfish pajamas. He'd get in big trouble if he sicced Garf on me.

"Sorry lady, we're a wholesale operation," Whip says. "We don't sell to the public."

"We're not here for *traps*," Aunt Blanche says disdainfully. "We're looking for my niece's lost cat."

Whip shrugs. "Can't help ya. Haven't seen any cats."

He doesn't look us in the eyes. It's obvious he's lying, but due to his dark, evil, trash-can heart, he just doesn't want to be helpful.

"Do you mind if we take a peek inside your building? Cats are great at hiding," Aunt Blanche says. "I had a friend whose cat hid in her pot belly lemonade pitcher for three days."

Then Poppy's aunt does something that impresses me further. She climbs out of her car and marches toward the doors like she knows he'll open them.

"I've got a big shipment to put together. But you can look for a couple of minutes, I guess," Whip tells us, rolling open the big doors. That's when I see Old Poppy.

"Mitten Man!" I cry, racing toward her as she hurries out of the shop.

But what I see next is a total tragedy, comedy, and drama at once. Old Poppy sprints headfirst toward a sticky spider trap. Incredibly, just in time, a box inches forward in front of Mitten Man, sticking itself to the gluey trap. How did it do that? *Thwump!*

"That's not good," Aunt Blanche says. Using lightning-quick reflexes that I didn't realize she had, Aunt Blanche lifts off the box with one hand and scoops up Raul with the other.

"It's very dangerous to put sticky traps out like this," Aunt Blanche tells Whip. "Look what you've done."

Raul and I lock eyes and I try to tell him what's what. "Don't freak out. I'm Mitten Man. The lady who's holding you isn't going to hurt you. We're here to rescue everybody."

I think Raul understands what I'm saying. I can tell by the freaked-out look on his face. He always pretends to be much more relaxed than he actually is.

"That cat and turtle are total jerks. Look at the mess they made of my delivery stack," Whip says. "It's gonna take an hour for me to sort and pile these again."

"That's nothing. Here's a real catastrophe," Aunt Blanche says, gently lifting and rotating Raul so Whip can see how all four of the turtle's feet are pasted tight to the cardboard strip. "How are you going to help this turtle?"

"Lady, you seem like you've got some free time," Whip says very perceptively. "Why don't *you* help that turtle."

"Oh, I will," she says. "Let's get out of here, Poppy."

I look around for Old Poppy, but she's . . . gone. Wait, what? I'm shocked. Doesn't she want her old life back? What happens if this curse has some sort of time limit? I don't want to stay in this body long enough to experience any of sixth grade! What a nightmare.

Aunt Blanche drives us home, and I look deeply into the passing fields for any sign of Old Poppy. Day after day after day, when I was a cat, Old Poppy loved me so hard. No matter what was going on inside her busy life, I always felt like her center. Now she won't even let me see her, let alone hold her. Not once, but twice she's leapt back into the wilderness instead of coming with me. Maybe I should carry snack food with me at all times. I could make a kit of her favorite things to remind her that she belongs with me and lure her back into my arms. It would be easy to keep something like that in my backpack. Isn't it worth a try?

We turn down our road and I can see with my eyeballs that we're almost home, but it doesn't feel how it should. Until Old Poppy comes back, our house will have an Old Poppy–shaped hole in it. And that thing feels much, much bigger than it looks.

CHAPTER 18

Don't Believe Your Eyeballs

I did not expect any of that to happen. Wow. Did Big Poppy show up at the spider building with Aunt Blanche? Did Raul just walk into a glue trap? Were those my jellyfish pajamas Big Poppy had on? If that's how she dresses to storm a spider building, what kind of fashion choices is she making to go to school?! My mind spins trying to process the drama. Big Poppy flung her arms out like she expected me to jump into them. Of course I couldn't leave with her. I need to get back to Death Tiger!

Too bad Raul isn't with me to convince him to go to the vet. I bet it will shock his ears straight that most of my plan actually worked.

But as I approach the spot where I left Death Tiger, I'm disturbed by what I see. Nothing. It's a patch of empty flat grass.

Once, Heni and I got separated at the mall. At first I thought she'd gone to the jewelry kiosk, but I was wrong. So I tried to find her in the bathroom. She wasn't there either. I felt so panicked, because the rule when we're at the mall is we need to stick together. But then I saw her walking toward me carrying a lemonade with paper bendy straws.

I don't know Death Tiger well enough yet to try to guess where he'd be. Maybe like in that situation, things aren't as bad as they seem. Maybe something good is actually happening. Maybe he went to the vet on his own.

"You know the truth will break your heart.

You know it was his time to part."

Are the grasshoppers trying to tell me that Death Tiger is dead? I mean, I know they're very negative insects, but did they see something? If they did, and if he's gone, shouldn't there be some sign of a fight?

"The fur you have right now will be

your fur for all eternity."

What?! Is that really how life works? It can't be. I still have the collar. We can still switch back. I walk over to the ground where I left Death Tiger. Oddly, it still feels warm.

"Where's Raul?" a weak voice asks.

I can't see anybody. This could be a trap. Maybe weasels are so weaselly that they throw their voices like ventriloquists.

"Mitten Man?" the soft voice whispers.

It sounds like Death Tiger. I inch my way deep into a patch of yellow weeds. "Hello?"

Out of the darkness, Death Tiger's face appears. He crawls toward me and falls at my feet. "The weasels are coming," he says. His eyes look dull and I can see his rib bones.

"Where? I'll save you!" I flatten out my back. Weasels are killing machines. That's what Death Tiger said, anyway. If we've got time to escape them, we should do that. "Let's go back to my house." If Big Poppy rescued Raul, she'll take care of us too. I have a lot of complicated feelings when it comes to Big Poppy, but it's our only chance. Death Tiger blinks his fragile gray eyes at me.

"Just go without me," he says weakly.

"What about the weasels?" I ask.

Death Tiger closes his eyes. Twigs snap.

"Up!" I tell him.

244

We need to move. I can feel it in my bones that we're not safe here. I head-butt him seven times, until he finally lifts his hind legs and walks. I can see a light on at a house. I want to run toward it, but Death Tiger can't go any faster. As we inch along, there's a new terrifying smell in the air. The weasels *are* getting closer.

"The worst is on its way to you.

There's not a thing that you can do."

Are the grasshoppers right? It kind of feels like they're rooting for bad things to happen to me. In all my life, I've never felt so unsafe. And not just for me, but for my friend. As we approach the backyard of the house with the light on, I spot the thing I've been dreading more than anything in the world: a long neck and twitching nose.

"Down," I whisper. Death Tiger and I press our bodies flat into the weeds. I'm terrified. If I try to fight a weasel, it could crush my skull and eat my brains. But I don't want that thing to kill Death Tiger either. We need to stay hidden. To stay as still as possible, I hold my breath.

"A weasel has it out for you.

All it wants to do is chew."

It sniffs for something. Can it smell us? I want so badly to close my eyes, to make things go dark and quiet my fear. But I can't lose track of it. I watch the weasel's every move.

As it moves toward our weedy hiding spot, I can't believe my eyeballs. It's almost as if the weasel turns into liquid. All fluid, it pivots and flies fast through the air, and a high-pitched squeal crashes into my ears. Oh, gross, the weasel has something in its teeth! I look to make sure Death Tiger is still beside me. Then the weasel speeds away fast, knocking against the yellow weeds, leaving a mist of golden pollen in its dust.

"A mouse right now, a cat for later.
Your danger grows from great to greater."

These grasshoppers might be super doomy, but they're also somewhat accurate. That weasel will be back. Isn't that something Death Tiger told me about weasels? After one finds a food source, it returns again and again. We can't be hanging around these mice-infested parts. We gotta go.

"I forgot my Frisbee!"

The soft, calm sound of a familiar boy's voice lands in my ears. Death Tiger and I inch toward the house. It's my Hot

Seat partner: Max! He's grabbed a Frisbee and runs back inside. I know what I need to do. Using my front paws, I wiggle my collar off my neck. Then I gently slide it over Death Tiger's head.

"Go to the back door," I tell him. "Max is nice. His family will take care of you."

Death Tiger scratches at the collar, trying to take it off.

"You'll need that," I say. "Raul might have been right. If they think you're a stray, they might not treat you as well. If they think somebody owns you, they'll take better care of you. They'll call my family. They'll take you to a vet. They'll get you what you need."

"No," Death Tiger says.

It's almost as if he can tell how important that collar is to me.

"I'll meet you back at my house," I say. "Everything is going to be okay."

I watch, at peace, as Death Tiger staggers to Max's back door. I worry he'll collapse on the welcome mat and nobody will see him. So I release the deepest cat cry I can muster. "Meow! Meow! Meow!"

As Max comes to his back patio door, I remember what an excellent Hot Seat partner he was. He never got upset if I missed a question, and he was a marvelous speller. Also, he wore really fun light-up shoes. Watching him discover Death Tiger reminds me that I do miss fifth-graders. Not just being one, but being surrounded by them. He calls to his parents, and all three of them crouch down and tenderly inspect my friend's wound. Max lifts up the tag on his collar and reads it. They gather Death Tiger in a towel and take him inside. If it's possible to save him, I know they will. Good people try to do good things.

CHAPTER 19

Disaster, Disaster, Disaster

I can't imagine a worse reaction to showing up at home after missing school with a glue-disaster turtle. I mean, Poppy's parents are beyond furious.

"What we have here is an epic catastrophe," Marlena says.

She has her laptop open, searching for solutions on how to dislodge Raul from the glue trap. It's an hours-long saga unfolding in our kitchen. She tried using vegetable oil, but in his current condition Raul doesn't want to be lightly massaged and gently tugged. He's a snapper. Poppy's parents have gone through probably a thousand paper towels and an entire tub of wet wipes, and he's still ninety percent pasted to the trap.

"We just need to go to the vet," Aunt Blanche says. "Don't worry about the money. I'll pay for it. I'll take any opportunity to contribute my share of humanity's debt to animals."

Marlena bubbles with anger, as if she's made of lava. Turn her loose and this woman could melt the earth.

"Humanity's debt?! *You* caused all of this!" Marlena spurts. "If you hadn't released Poppy's beloved pet into the wild, none of us would be in this predicament *and* Poppy wouldn't have an unexcused absence!"

"I'm opening up my wallet to fix it," says Aunt Blanche. Her supreme calmness is sending Marlena into full geysers of rage.

All this arguing makes me feel super glum. "I think I'll wait in my room," I say.

Raul gives me another wicked stare, which makes no sense, because I've been a tremendous ally for him during this whole mess. It feels like I'm getting blamed for every stinking problem in east Idaho these days. I turn to leave.

"Don't get too attached, because we are not keeping that turtle," Don says. "It clearly belongs to somebody."

"Well, whoever owns it is a monster, because they're spraying it purple," Aunt Blanche says. "Everybody knows that paint kills turtles."

Poppy's parents exchange a look.

"Listen," Marlena says to me, "what you and Aunt Blanche did today is outrageous and wrong. She didn't have permission to let you miss school and look for Mitten Man."

"And going to look for your cat at a spider trap shop while still in your pajamas also is inexplicable to us," Don says.

I look down at my jellyfish jammies. They look almost like daytime clothes to me. I don't see the big deal.

I can't let them continue to trample me with their loud objections. I *know* what I did today was the *right* thing to do. "Excuse me," I interrupt. "Let's not overlook the fact that today we saved a turtle, *and* I would have saved Mitten Man except he got spooked and ran away, so our 'outrageous behavior' was almost a gigantic success. And shouldn't that be our real goal in life? To live gigantic successful days?"

Poppy's parents exchange another look. They appear to be on the verge of losing it completely.

"Blanche," Marlena says sternly. "Come with me. Poppy, you and Dad are going to stay here and discuss what we learned today talking to your principal."

Holy wombat boogers. It's tragic to think that while I was out living my gigantic successful day, things I did earlier in the week were dooming me. That's the real downside of being a fifth grader. It's hard to shake the consequences of what you do in school with so many tattletale eyeballs on you. And yes, I'm including Ms. Gish in that assessment. When Old Poppy and I switch back, if we switch back, I hope she can forgive me, because even though I tried to do my best, I fear, if I'm being absolutely honest, that I made her life much, much, much, much, much, much, much worse.

I don't even have time to argue with what Marlena said. She's out the door along with Aunt Blanche. Don sits on the couch and rubs his temples, like he has a life-obliterating headache. That's when I spot a bug so evil I reflexively take off my slipper and try to whack it.

"Whoa! Spider?" Don asks.

"Worse. A grasshopper. Where do we keep the bug poison? For one to make it inside the house, we probably have an infestation out back." I shake my head. "And doomsayers don't bunk in my house. Not on my watch."

Don sighs. "We aren't going to bug-bomb the backyard at night because of a grasshopper."

With his hands, he gently cups the green invader and sets him outside.

"Fine. Now that we've taken care of that, who do we call in this town to report a dangerous dog?" I blurt out.

"We're not going to do that either," Don says.

"Well, what are we going to do?" I ask. I feel very pumped up and motivated to do something.

"The dishes," Don says with a scowl. "Meet me at the sink."

That comment makes my eyes bug out. It's super lame to do household chores during a life crisis. Don must know that.

Cleaning silverware with Don is a surprisingly unpleasant experience. He's so mad about everything that the energy feels tense and the only thing he wants to talk about is my "errant" school behavior and friendship problems.

"When did you and Heni stop eating lunch together?"

"Can you explain again why you climbed that tree?"

"Why did you award a student in your class fifty thousand points?"

At first, I ignore him and focus on scrubbing between all the fork tines. But the questions keep rolling at me like out-of-control kickballs. I realize he's going to keep badgering me until I give him a good answer.

"Heni is a problematic friend," I say. "I tripped on the puke bucket and she didn't even help me up. She stood by silently while the whole entire school laughed at me."

"When did this happen?" he asks.

"Last week," I say.

"That seems like something you should've mentioned to us," he says.

"Well, I struck out and found other friends. Eighth graders. We're making cookies to sell to help mistreated animals or something. And maybe I'm helping design a website too. It feels like a cause I can get behind."

I've scrubbed hard enough on one of the drinking glasses that I removed a painted bee. Don grabs a towel.

"Your friendship with Heni seems like something worth saving," he says. "Even best friends make mistakes."

I think about what he's saying. "So you're telling me I should forgive anybody who stomps on my heart?"

Don thinks before he answers. "Would you want Heni to forgive you?"

I shrug. That's a tough question. If I'm thinking like a cat, I don't care. People are everywhere. If things go bad with one, you can find another.

But if I'm thinking like Old Poppy, I guess I do care. Heni tries hard to be a good friend. You shouldn't flush everything down the toilet because one bad thing happened between you.

"She did apologize seven times," I say.

"That means something. Doesn't it?"

Before I can answer that question, his phone rings. "I can't believe it! You've got Mitten Man! You need to shave the leg? Lance it? Flush it? Yes! Do whatever you need to do. We'll be right there."

Don clicks off the call and hugs me so tightly that I can feel his heart beating.

"Let's go!" he says.

I'm super excited to learn we've found Mitten Man but deeply perturbed to learn I'm getting my leg fur shaved— for a second time in my short life. When it grows back, it

255

itches like crazy. I mean, I'm never going to be able to stop licking the bald spot. Maybe I can convince Poppy to stay a cat till it's long again.

On the way there Don asks me to text Marlena where we're going, so I attempt to do this. But I've never texted anybody before. Turns out I've got slippery thumbs. I accidentally send the text to somebody named Bengte.

"Oops. I sent it to Bengte," I say.

"Bengte is our jury foreperson!" Don explains. "Don't trouble her with this."

"Too late," I say.

"Just copy that text and send it to your mother," he says.

"Oops," I say. "That one went to Brian."

"Brian Evenson?" he asks.

I tap the info button. "Yes."

"Hand me back my phone," he says. "That's our plumber."

This whole interaction makes me feel so much better about lobbying for a four-story cat tower with a sisal rope for Old Poppy's birthday present. Having a phone would be such a burden. Think of all the wrong numbers Old Poppy might accidentally dial. Think of all the people who might accidentally misdial her. She doesn't need to be pestered like that. Clearly, phones create a bunch of problems. I'm seriously proud that I'm the reason Old Poppy will not be getting a birthday phone.

I watch out the window as we whiz underneath beaming streetlights. Maybe when Old Poppy and I reunite, it will become clear how to switch back. Maybe she'll look at me and I'll look at her and we'll know exactly what we need to say. I'm so excited and breathing so much that I fog my window. With my pointer finger I trace a big heart on the cool glass. How much longer will I have to deal with these hands?

You'd think suddenly turning into a fifth grader after being a cat for your whole life would automatically cause a deep change in how you thought about everything. But that wasn't how it happened. I think the big change for me came when Old Poppy ran away from me. Not just once, but twice. I didn't realize how much I liked her until she didn't want to be in my life with me. If I wanted to tell her something, I couldn't. If I craved a quick cuddle, the only thing in my bed was empty space.

This is what I've come to believe: Old Poppy was like a little flame. She gave off warmth and light and energy. And when she left, all that turned into a bunch of nothingness. And I didn't realize it until it was too late.

I don't realize I'm wearing my slippers until I'm standing outside the vet's office and see myself reflected in the front door's glass. Don swings open the front door and I follow him inside. Mom and Aunt Blanche look so surprised when they see us. They just think they're saving Raul. They don't even know they've found Old Poppy.

"They've got Mitten Man too!" Don says. "They just called me."

Marlena jumps to her feet. "That's amazing!"

Aunt Blanche kisses her hand and tosses it into the air. "Thank the heavens!" she says.

We gather at the front desk. There's a bell on it so I ding it.

"You don't need to ding it," Don says. "They saw us come in."

But I don't regret ringing that bell at all, because it's probably the last bell I'll ever ding.

"Here's Mitten Man," a cheerful woman says, bringing out a large orange cat cradled in a blue towel. "He's doing well enough that you can take him home tonight."

It's absolutely shocking to see Death Tiger wearing Old Poppy's collar. What happened? Where's my owner?

"That's not Mitten Man," Marlena says. "Why would you think that's our cat?"

The cheerful woman grows startled and checks the cat's collar again.

"That's his collar all right," Don says. "But that's not our cat."

"Who brought in the cat?" Marlena asks.

"A good Samaritan who found him on his porch," she says. "We called your husband to go over the injuries."

"Well, this certainly took an unexpected turn," Aunt Blanche says. "We might end up with one cat and one turtle to take home tonight. *Both* complete strangers to us!"

"We're not taking home two animals tonight," Don says. "We're not running a shelter. No offense."

A slightly more cheerful man enters the lobby holding Raul, who looks damp and unhappy, but at least he's been de-glued.

"You can't take this turtle home with you," he says. "He's got a chip. We gathered his information from it and contacted his owners in Sun Valley. He's been missing for almost an entire year! They're making plans to fly him home."

I am shook. Raul gets to ride in an airplane home? What a waste. Nothing about him says aviation-curious at all.

"Wow," Aunt Blanche says. "That's a beautiful reptile. I hope his owners appreciate him."

Out of nowhere, I feel something I've never felt before. My face grows warm and tears burn behind my eyeballs. I hear my own sobs before I understand that I'm crying.

"It's okay," Poppy's mother says, holding me. "It's going to be okay."

"But it's not," I say. "My cat is probably gone forever."

I know Big Poppy would not have parted with that magic collar lightly. It feels like she's sending me a message. I mean, it's the one thing she needed to return to her life. Which tells me that: either she's dead, or she's totally over me as a friend. Is this how it ends? I take the deepest breath of my life. I guess it is. This is what I have now. I look at Don and Marlena and Death Tiger through tear-blurred eyes.

"How much do I owe you?" Aunt Blanche says. "I'd like to take the orange cat with the bad leg home."

Aunt Blanche whips out her credit card and settles the debt—just Death Tiger's, not all of humanity's at the moment. The collar feels light and flimsy in my hands. What am I supposed to do with this? Keep it and look at it every day? Wonder when Old Poppy will come home, when she'll probably never come home at all? Why would I want to keep something that's brought me so much sadness and bad luck? Not only did this collar ruin my entire life, it probably ended Old Poppy's very existence. I hate this thing! I throw it into the small trash can by the door.

I'm so sad and angry that I start sweating like mad, even behind my knees. I stomp out to the car and throw myself in Don's passenger seat. My life has given me a lot of terrible news in the last five minutes. What do I do now?

CHAPTER 20

A Sneaky Way

I walk the alfalfa fields for the last time. It's not safe for me out here. Dogs, owls, weasels, skunks, and everything else in this darkness seem eager to chew me up. Whether I'm ready or not, it's time to go home.

It occurs to me as I pick my path that maybe I made a terrible mistake. Everything will be fine if Mom and Dad and Big Poppy come to the vet and get Death Tiger. They'll see it's the wrong cat, but Big Poppy will figure it out and demand that Death Tiger come with them. Right? But what happens if Death Tiger doesn't make it? What if Hot Seat Max just decides to keep him and ignore the worried family waiting on the other side of that collar? What happens to my collar then? What happens to me?

Worst case, I can get Big Poppy to steal back the collar from Max's house, or something. As long as we have the collar, I know we'll be able to find a way back to who we really are. I want to stay hopeful. I want to believe my plan will work out. So I'll use my last moments of animal freedom to do something I'll never be able to do again.

Kit's house isn't far from this field. I'll race there first. Eventually, Big Poppy and I will figure out how to switch back, and before that happens, I should know where I stand with everyone, and get a sense of where I'll belong.

I've actually only been to Kit's house once, for a Halloween party last year. We watched a scary movie about a boy who made a Frankenstein monster using his old toys and Heni and I got so freaked out that we boxed up our old toys and stacked them in our basements the next day. It had been a fun night though. Kit's mom made us pickle dip and Kit's dad kept trying to scare us by making spooky noises. Kit held her hedgehog, Beebo, tucked in his snuggle sack, through the entire movie and didn't let anybody else in the room touch him, except when Kit wasn't looking Rosario sneakily pet him at least a dozen times.

I leap onto the ledge of Kit's bedroom window. Kit is in there with a girl I don't recognize from behind. They've got fast music playing and they're dancing. It's not like a fun dance, like two people having a good time, but a hard dance. They're each doing the same moves over and over like it's their job. Who is that girl? When she finally turns around, it's Pepper! I press my face close to the window's glass to hear what they're saying.

"If I can rock this routine and prove to Ms. Dance that I'm as good as you," Kit says, "she'll have to let me be a pony."

Pepper looks unconvinced. "I don't think that's how school plays work. You might be in denial, you know. Maybe we should practice your dog moves too, just in case."

"I am not a dog!" Kit shouts.

The music starts up again. They kick, stomp, criss-cross, arm whip, twist, punch, shoulder wiggle, shuffle, back-up hop, and power kick. Kit looks fine as always, but Pepper's moves are spectacular. I should be watching her bop and whirl on TV during a football game halftime show. When she breaks out the swisher arms, I realize she's using some of my power moves too. This is amazing. Deep down I guess she really did admire my fresh style.

"Okay," Pepper says. "I think I need to go."

"Wait! Wait! I'm not ready to give up," Kit says.

"Here's the thing," Pepper says. "Dancing makes you mean, and I do it for fun."

"I can't have fun until I'm better at it!" Kit says.

"I'll see you at school," Pepper says.

She slips out of Kit's room. And instead of cuddling Beebo, or reading a book, or calling a friend, Kit practices her dance moves again and again. It's like she's broken. I've never seen anybody so determined to be a pony.

A cold wind cuts across my fur and I hop down from the windowsill, hurrying along the fence line until I get to Rosario's backyard. She's outside jumping her Skip-It on the back patio, wearing her fringe vest. With each hop the tassels flip and fly.

We always teased her about that Skip-It. But I don't know why. *Swish. Click. Swish. Click.* Watching her now, it looks like fun. Her happiness spills out of her. I miss Rosario, even though I didn't spend much time with her outside the clump. I did go mini-golfing with her once, and she knocked her ball into the same water hazard four times.

265

Watching that putt-putt worker wade into that miniature plaster Taj Mahal over and over cracked us both up so hard we had trouble holding our clubs steady after that. Now I wish I'd spent more time trying to get to know her instead of obsessing over impressing Kit.

By the time I make it to Heni's house, she's already in her pajamas. I watch as she takes a tube of fish food off her desk and scatters flakes for her dwarf gourami, Ariana. Wait a minute. There are two fish in the bowl. The blue pair flit around each other to snap up the briny flakes. Wow. Heni got a new pet.

A tiny pain stabs me. Who am I kidding? Take away Poppy McBean and everybody's life skips merrily along. Right now I feel closer to Heni than I ever have, and she doesn't even know I'm here. When's the last time she thought of me?

As I race through the dew-dampened grass I realize I'm not furious with Big Poppy anymore. She did a lousy job at being me for sure. But what does it matter? Being Mitten Man came with its own set of problems: helping out Death Tiger, having to avoid skunks and outsmart weasels.

Being alive is hard work no matter who you are. At least Big Poppy swooped in when it mattered. Even the way she treated Heni, I realize, was because she was mad at Heni on my behalf. I feel a little warm glow. She actually does care about me.

Pit. Pat. Pit. Pat. I've walked so much tonight that my paws feel tender. No. This isn't how I imagined my life turning out, but I'm not going to be mad about it.

When I get to my house all the lights are off. That's weird since tomorrow is a school day and too early for everybody to be asleep. I look in the windows but can't see anything except for the bright blue lights of electronics charging. Where has everybody gone? Did they go out to dinner? That's the only thing that makes sense. They probably went to the Snakebite. Mom and Dad love their Teton burger and I always get the Snakebite quesadilla, though who knows what Big Poppy did to that tradition. I wonder if they took Aunt Blanche?

The moon hangs over the night, casting a pink glow so bright it could almost warm the ground. My bones throb from the day's chaos and bad luck, and I curl up in a patch of yarrow beside our patio. I haven't eaten hot food in days. I grill a quesadilla in my mind and mentally taste the gooey cheese. Soon, Big Poppy will help me fix all our problems. Soon, I'll be back with my family where I belong.

CHAPTER 21

No Luck

Carrying Death Tiger into my bedroom makes me miss Old Poppy more than words can say. I mean, Death Tiger is a perfectly fine cat, but he's not Old Poppy. He's not the person who's raised me since I was a kitten. I'd give everything I had to bring her back. Aunt Blanche throws an arm around me.

"Life is so funny," she says. "You lose one cat and you gain another all in the same night."

Hot tears burn behind my eyeballs. That's not how I feel about things at all.

"It's late, sweetheart," Marlena says. "You should go to bed."

"Yeah," I say.

"You shouldn't sleep with the new cat," Aunt Blanche says. "What if he's a scratcher? Safer to let him spend his first night in the bathroom. I can spritz some relaxing chamomile spray on the shower curtain. That'll Zen everything."

I look down at Death Tiger. He's probably never even seen a bathroom before.

Don takes him from my arms. "We'll put some food, water, and the litter box in there for him too. Aunt Blanche is right on this one."

For once! "When are you leaving again?" I ask. I don't mean to be rude, but I'm ready for my life to return to having one borrowed mom and one borrowed dad and zero difficult hippie aunts.

"We decided she's heading out tomorrow morning," Marlena says.

"I think I've done all I can do here," Aunt Blanche says.

Truer words were never spoken.

I let Aunt Blanche hug me good night and goodbye and then I hurry to the spare room. Since I'm in my pajamas, and the foldout couch is already made up, I should crawl straight into bed. But I don't. I go to the closet and move a stack of file boxes out of the corner. Then I curl up in the smallest place I can fit.

I've never felt this kind of heartache before. Normally when I press myself into a small space I automatically feel safe and relaxed. But no matter which way I turn I keep thinking about Old Poppy. Elephants mourn over the bones of their loved ones. Mother seals cry out when killer whales snap up their young. Cats crawl under a couch and we turn our backs to pain. Why am I still crying? What's happening to me? There's so much sadness inside of me, and nowhere for me to put it.

I squeeze my eyes shut as tight as I can. But regrets bubble up. I should've come home and warned Old Poppy about Aunt Blanche right away. I should've taken a flashlight. I should've used my long fleshy arms and grabbed her at the spider trap compound. What good are having hands if you don't use them to catch runaway animals?

Human bodies are so weird. I'm so sad that I begin to hear imaginary sounds. I grab a pillow and put it over my head, but I can still hear the soft meows of Old Poppy. Is this how it'll be from now on? My lost-forever owner haunts me from the great beyond, as a cat?

I take my pillow off my head. Those meows sound very real. I crawl out of the closet and walk to the window.

Under the pink light of a bright full moon, sitting on my window is . . . Old Poppy!!! Holy badger scat. I was wrong! Old Poppy isn't gone. Happiness rips through me so hard that I start dancing. How is this happening? How can Old Poppy be alive and well? I yank open my window and smell her dusty fur through the screen.

"You're here!" I say.

"And very, very tired," Old Poppy says.

I grab my backpack equipped with my Old Poppy preparedness kit, race out of my room and down the hallway, and rip open the front door. At my feet sits a tiny beast I never thought I'd see again. I pick her up and hold her close. I don't even need to break out my kit. Her little heart thunders inside her chest and she instantly begins to purr.

"When you were lost out there, I missed you every second you were gone," I say. "And when I thought you weren't coming back, my heart broke into a zillion hurt pieces. I don't want you to ever go away again." And then I scream so loud I'm sure I shake the trees. "I LOVE YOU!"

"Are you okay?" Heni asks.

I shoot her a very surprised look. Where did Heni even come from? Why is she in my yard?

"I heard you screaming and wanted to check on you," she says.

It's like she can read my mind. I lift Mitten Man up to show her.

"That's amazing!" she cheers. "You found him!"

"Not quite. He found me. Do you want to come in?" I ask Heni.

She hesitates. "I'm actually supposed to be in bed."

I reach into my backpack and pull out the note Old Poppy and I wrote to apologize to Heni. It's not perfect, but it's something.

"I'm sorry," I say. And maybe I should say something else, but I'm not sure what it should be.

"Okay," Heni says. "Thanks."

She takes the note and turns and leaves and I watch the back of her head. There goes a world-class friend, who also happens to have very wavy and attractive hair. I'm sure I've still got a long way to go to repair Old Poppy's friendship with Heni, but at least things are on a better path than they were five minutes ago.

I bring Old Poppy into the living room and set her down on the floor. Her rib and hip bones poke out under her fur.

Old Poppy responds with a series of meows.

I look into her tired eyes. "Let's catch up tomorrow."

She nods her sweet furry head. "All I want to do is sleep in my bed."

"You do not want to sleep in your bed," I say. "There's a special guest in it. You want to sleep with me on the pullout couch."

I clutch Old Poppy close and walk us back to the office where I sleep, then crawl into the pullout couch. It's never been so cozy. All the sadness has been replaced with a new feeling. Pure calm. I hold Old Poppy and feel her breath on my neck. Curled into a ball, she warms a spot above my heart, making me feel a peace so deep that I want to stay like this for days.

"What happened to Death Tiger?" Old Poppy asks with a yawn.

"Oh, he's in the bathroom. Aunt Blanche is afraid he's a vicious beast," I explain.

"Well, he is and he isn't," Old Poppy says. "Cats are so much more complicated than people think."

I can feel Old Poppy's body soften as she slips into sleep. I don't try to keep talking to her. We have plenty of time for that. I mean, maybe Don and Marlena will be soft-hearted enough to let me stay home from school tomorrow so I can re-bond with my cat. Wouldn't that be amazing? I could avoid another drama-filled day as a fifth grader. It might be a day of one hundred percent pure Old Poppy.

• • • • •

The spot where Old Poppy sleeps next to me is still blazing hot. Her life out there must have exhausted her. It's unusual for a cat to sleep past dawn like this. But here she is, furiously purring beside me, right where she belongs. I give her a loving pet and a quick kiss before I climb out of bed. Then I carefully pick out a shirt that I know she'll like.

Old Poppy yawns so wide I see all of her molars plus her tonsils. "You cannot wear that shirt!" she says to me, hopping off the pullout couch and performing a giant back stretch.

I'm so surprised I make a weird gasping sound. "You wear this shirt all the time! And you love unicorns," I say, pointing to its color-flipping sequin horn.

"That's my Heni-matching shirt," Old Poppy explains. "I only wear it on days when she wears it. It's something we have to coordinate. If Heni sees me in that shirt, she'll think I'm sending her a secret message that I want our friendship to be dunzo. And I do *not* want to send that message to her!" she says. "We can't make things worse with my friends. You saw Heni last night. I've still got a chance to mend stuff."

I don't even try to argue with Old Poppy even though I'm not sure it's healthy for two eleven-year-olds to have any kind of unicorn-shirt agreement, and I change into a green sweatshirt dress with rabbits on it. I'm dreading telling her that I threw away her collar. It was the absolute wrong thing to do. I understand that now. But at the time I thought Old Poppy was *gone* gone. The idea of looking at that collar every day crushed me. I want to believe at least a small part of her will understand, but I know she won't. I've probably ruined our lives in a very permanent way— *on accident.*

A brilliant idea pops into my head and I go find Don.

He's in the kitchen drinking a monster-size cup of coffee. "Good thing we put that orange tiger cat in the bathroom. Look at this."

He wags his phone at me. It's a photo of a destroyed shower curtain, chewed-apart washcloth, and unwound toilet paper roll.

"There's even orange fur in the toothbrushes," Don says. "What a maniac."

Nothing about that photo looks Zen. "Wow," I say. "Aunt Blanche's spray had the opposite effect on that bathroom cat."

"Good point," Don says, taking another coffee gulp. "It invigorated him. Maybe I should spritz myself."

"Maybe," I say. But never in a million years would I voluntarily apply that misguided hippie's tinctures to my body. "So, I have an important question. Can we call the vet?" I keep my voice so soft he has to lean down to hear me. "I threw away Mitten Man's collar last night, because I thought he wasn't coming back and the thought of looking at that particular thing for the rest of my life completely torpedoed all my joy. But now I really, really need it back."

"Well, I'm supposed to call the office and update them on that orange tiger cat," he says. "I'll ask. They probably still have it."

Hearing Don say that reassures me. Basically, my problem is almost solved. So I really don't need to worry about anything. I return to my room to pick out a butterfly bead bracelet and run smack into Old Poppy.

"You threw the collar away?" she hisses. "Why would you do that?"

Her bright happy eyes are gone. Two tiny, rage-filled slits glare at me. I need to remember that cats have spectacularly good ears.

"Calm down," I say. "You heard Don. It'll probably be okay."

"*Probably?*" Old Poppy spits. "If we lose that collar, we're doomed!"

"I feel like you never congratulate me or thank me for any of the good stuff I've done. You know, I turned in your solar eclipse project many days late and you still got full credit and Ms. Gish hung it next to Heni's. You're welcome."

"What? I don't care about my solar eclipse art project! We need our collar!" Old Poppy says.

"Well, maybe this will make you feel better. I also donated your art project to Ms. Gish's daughter's kindergarten class so they can practice destroying paper with scissors. It was a very generous thing to do."

"Why are you still talking about my solar eclipse project? How are we supposed to switch back without my collar?" Old Poppy's eye-shouting now.

"The vet's office probably still has it," I say. "Who throws out the trash every day?"

"Uh, most places with a public trash can!"

Just then, Marlena yells, "You're going to miss the bus!"

The bus? Why are they suddenly making me ride the bus? I thought Poppy's parents loved her. I race to get all my books and papers together. It's like ever since I became a fifth grader the world has been raining problems down on me nonstop. I'm currently drenched with troubles, and I don't like it.

"I could drive her to school on the way out of town?" Aunt Blanche offers.

"No!" Poppy's parents shout in unison.

As I slam down breakfast, I hear the worst sound ever.

"Your cleaning crew already threw the trash out?" Don's saying into the phone. "Nobody saw anything? Okay, we'll order another collar," he says. "Thanks for looking."

I feel terrible as I slip on my backpack. I glance at Old Poppy. Her eyes have a gleam of complete despair in them that I've never seen before.

"I can see the bus!" Aunt Blanche says.

At least when I get home from school this very problematic and terrible aunt will be gone. Like a wildebeest following the seasonal rains during their long African migration, Aunt Blanche will loop back to California and complete this difficult journey that nearly destroyed us all. Hopefully, I won't see her again for a very, very, very, very long time.

"Oh, my wonderful, spicy niece, I hope to see you again very soon," Aunt Blanche gushes as she waves to me across the room and throws me air kisses, which I very deliberately do not catch.

Old Poppy watches me with the saddest eyes I've ever seen. I wish I had time to tell her the only thing I remember my mom ever telling me, long, long ago when I was a kitten, back when I lived on Carl's sweet farm where she cuddled me in a pile of hay. Mom always said, "Baby, you were born under a lucky star. You'll spend your whole life brightening the lives of others."

If I could explain to Old Poppy that my mother misled me and that my whole life I've been believing I had luck above me and luck below, when I probably had a lot less luck than that, maybe she'd understand why I did what I did. *I never thought I could make a choice that would end this badly.*

I aim a very loving gaze at Old Poppy. "We'll be okay," I tell her. But Old Poppy does not look reassured.

Aunt Blanche yells, "The bus is outside!"

Wow. Wow. Wow. Okay, I tell myself. This won't be hard. The bus will stop, I'll climb on board, and it'll be a short ride. Then, when I get to school, I'll enter my classroom and continue to pretend to learn. Year after year. Soon, I'll become a sixth grader. Then a seventh grader. Then I'll go to pizza-shop school and learn how to operate my own pizzeria. I'll bring Old Poppy to work with me every day. My whole life isn't over and neither is hers.

They're just going to be very, very different from what we thought we'd get.

CHAPTER 22
Box Heads

I wallow in despair on the couch and don't care about anything anymore. *Click. Clack. Click. Clack.* Sure, I hear Mom gathering all her stuff together in the kitchen. What does it matter? Before my life crashed into misery, I would have wanted to watch her get ready. Not me. Not now. Mom thinks I'm a nuisance. Out of nowhere, she appears above me and reaches down. Ack! Am I going to get tossed in the garage again?! No. She lovingly rubs between my ears.

"I missed you, rascal," she says, bending down to deliver a quick peck.

I look at her and tell her that I love her too. But she only hears meows. And then she's gone. That's the best I can hope for now. That my mother will not actively hate me and also occasionally pet or kiss me?

I trusted my cat, and look where it got me. Stuck as a cat! I return to my wallow spot on the couch. I'm so upset and stressed out that my fur starts falling out. Out of habit, I start licking. *Yoink!* I'm snatched into the air.

"I missed you too, furry fella," my dad says, cradling me in his arms.

When I look into his eyes, I can see my own reflection: a furry face staring right back at me. I need to get used to that image since apparently it's going to be my face for the rest of my life.

"I've done a final pass-through," Aunt Blanche booms, "and I think I got everything. Sage wand, check. Loofah, tarot deck, check, check. Cork yoga mat, check!"

My mother meets her by the front door. "You forgot your monk fruit sweetener."

Aunt Blanche flings her arms around my mom. "You're a goddess," she says, and then finally I hear the sweet sweet sound of house doors and then car doors slamming. I know this might sound mean, but I'm ridiculously happy to watch my enlightened aunt leave.

Next task: I go to the bathroom and check on Death Tiger.

"You gotta get me out of here," he says. "I wasn't built to live in a plastic crate."

He does look misplaced, tucked behind a metal mesh door, surrounded by piles of dirty clothes.

"You should've thought about that before you clawed apart the bathroom and destroyed our toilet paper," I say. I press my paw against the crate's mesh metal door. Death Tiger reaches out his paw and we gently touch them together.

"Are you really a fifth grader?" Death Tiger asks me.

It seems like an empty question. Because I'm not really that person anymore.

"I'm supposed to be," I say. "I mean, I used to be."

"So when do you turn back into the girl?"

I shake my head. "I don't think I do."

"What?" Death Tiger asks. "Why not?"

"Big Poppy threw the collar away," I say. "Without it, I can't turn back."

"There must be another way," Death Tiger says. "The collar didn't look *that* special. Maybe you can find another one."

"I don't think it works like that," I say. "That woman who paid for your treatment, my aunt, got it for me. She's a free-thinker who triggers calamity."

In all my eleven years I've only come across one magic collar. Chances are, even with Aunt Blanche's funky assistance, I won't live long enough to discover a second one. Especially as a cat.

"You're a good friend," Death Tiger tells me.

"Thanks," I say. In this moment hearing those words really means something to me.

Creak. Creak.

The sound of footsteps in the kitchen makes my fur stand on end. Everybody left. Who's there?

"Here, kitty-kitty."

I peek around the corner. It's Aunt Blanche! She must have doubled back and come in through the garage. She's going to either throw me out into the wilderness again, or take me back with her to California. Why else would she sneak into the house and come looking for me? I don't want to live in the boonies again, or Fresno! I run as fast as I can to Old Poppy's bedroom. I can hide way back in the closet. If I'm quiet enough maybe she'll—

"Gotcha!" Aunt Blanche says, snagging me by the back of the neck. She dangles me in front of her, like she's lovingly carrying a smelly bag of trash. "We need to have a talk."

285

I've been home less than a day, and now I'm going to be whisked away in the name of feline freedom. I look around, committing these walls to memory: the canvas of birch trees, Dad's family crest, our floral curtains Mom embroidered with bees, and our family photo where we all wore denim and posed in a pile of leaves in a meadow. Goodbye, life.

"I want to apologize for liberating you against your will," Aunt Blanche says. "And now I want to make it up to you."

She keeps one hand firmly on my neck as she reaches into her purse.

"People tease me about my love of trash cans and recycling bins, but I don't listen to them. There's a whole world of useful stuff that gets thrown out *before its time*."

I hear the tiny clink and ding of the blue quartz and silver moon trinket as Aunt Blanche gently wraps the slim white collar around my neck. *The collar.* Oh. My. Stars. Hope is not lost after all.

"I saw this in the trash at the vet's and it broke my heart. I always say, magic doesn't belong in a landfill with stinking diapers and thrown-out dolls. I bought this collar just for you. And crystals turn especially powerful when certain times are upon us, like the upcoming eclipse. It'll be our secret how this collar made its way back to you," Aunt Blanche says. "Everyone else will think it's magic. And in some ways, it is."

I take back every mean word I said about Aunt Blanche. Sometimes it's the people you least expect who deliver what you need. I can feel the heart and moon gently swinging against my neck fur.

"Now, I'd love to stay and chat, but I need to get on the road. I'm hoping to make it to Kelly Canyon to hike Gnarly Bear before the eclipse. I can't wait to stand on top of a mountain and experience wild totality." And with one more nice belly rub, she's gone.

After she leaves, a sense of urgency nags at me, and I don't know why. I should feel relief that I have the collar back, but instead I feel tense and fidgety. Maybe it's that I'm about to experience my first solar eclipse as a cat. I try to close my eyes, but my mind keeps thinking about switching back. It didn't work before, even *with* this collar. What do I need to do differently? I replay in my mind what happened. We wished our wishes. We were in the garage. Mitten Man sat in front of me on the cement.

Wait. He *wasn't* on the cement. He was on construction paper. He was on my solar eclipse project! I think back to galaxy glitter chalk and the circle I drew. I accidentally set Mitten Man on that when he scratched me. That's it! I need to sit on my art project when I make my wish. That's the thing we'd forgotten about!

I race around the house very thrilled. I skitter across the tile floor. I end up banging into Death Tiger's crate.

"You got your collar back," Death Tiger says. "Wow."

"I know!" I cheer. "Now all I need is for Big Poppy to bring home my art project and we can switch back! Who knew a fifth-grade art assignment could be so important?"

"Wait," Death Tiger says. "The art project you and Big Poppy fought over this morning?"

I'm so happy I don't follow what he's saying. "We weren't really fighting. I was just upset about the collar."

"But didn't she say she was giving your art project away?"

Holy kamoley. I need that art project! Does it even exist anymore or has it been chopped into pieces by clumsy kindergartners? I work to slow down my breathing. Ms. Gish always takes art down after an event is over, and the event is happening right now. If I can get to the school right now, I can fix my life. But if I don't, I will be a cat until I die. I'm in the wrong place at exactly the wrong time.

I race to the kitchen window. Using my front paws, I knock out the wooden dowel, pull, and heave. It's a long way down to the cement patio. I hold my breath and leap. And I'm out!

I know which road to follow to get to the school. As long as I'm careful and stay on the turfy shoulder, I think I'll be safe. I race at top speeds. I jump over a gopher. I pass a chipmunk. I power through clumps of hawkweed, knapweed, and Scotch broom. I have one goal: get to Upper Teton Middle School, find my solar eclipse art project, get Big Poppy, and get in position.

When I look up I can see the sun sliding toward the moon. The eclipse is today. Is it possible Ms. Gish has already taken the art projects down?

I'm almost to school when I hear the chatter of students. What a relief. The warning bell hasn't rung yet. Big Poppy might still be outside too. I leap across the front yard and thread through a few legs. I don't see Big Poppy anywhere. Rosario.

Yes. Deezil. Unfortunately. There's only one thing left to do. I bound up the front steps and race past the hall monitor. I make a left turn at the trophy case and head to Ms. Gish's class.

"Is that cat supposed to be here?" a fourth grader asks as she pulls a book from her locker.

"Dunno," her friend replies, fluffing her hair. "Maybe it's here for play practice."

Ha! If only they knew about this cat and play practice. But I don't have time to stop and teach them eyeball-speech. As I approach Ms. Gish's classroom, my heart flutters faster than a billion butterflies set loose at once. Ah, I've missed this place. My friends. My teacher. My desk. My life. I spot Big Poppy talking to Heni in the book corner. They look like they're having a serious conversation. The last thing I want to do is interrupt her, but I must.

"How can you be a cat?" Heni asks. "You *have* been acting strange. But a cat? That seems impossible."

"Yeah, you can't be logical about this, Heni. What's happened to me is beyond that," Big Poppy says. "Look at how I move."

Out of nowhere, she busts out a cartwheel and lands in the splits.

Heni gasps. "But, Poppy, you can't do a cartwheel or the splits!"

"Exactly. It's called feline flexibility. Believe your eyeballs, Heni. I'm not really Poppy," Big Poppy says.

"Meow. Meow. Meow," I interrupt.

"Is it you?!" Heni shouts. "Poppy?!"

"*Poppy?!*" Big Poppy cries. "This is bananas! You shouldn't be here!"

Why hasn't she noticed the collar yet? I ram into her legs until she picks me up. That's when she feels it, and she looks me in the eye.

"How did you get it?" Big Poppy asks.

"It doesn't matter. You need to take down my solar eclipse art project. That's the thing we forgot. You were on top of it when we made our wishes," I say. "I think it's the missing piece to fixing everything."

Big Poppy seems stunned. "You want me to rip it down? Right now?"

"Yes!" I say.

"That's crazy," Big Poppy says. "It'll leave a big blank space. Ms. Gish will ask me about it. Here's a different idea: How about I take it down right as we leave for the solar eclipse. Then I'll take you with me when we all go outside."

Big Poppy winks at me. That's when I remember I forgot to

wink at Heni. I promised her in my note that when she saw

me I'd wink at her.

Wink. Wink. Wink.

"I believe you," Heni says. "You don't need to keep wink-

ing at me, Poppy."

Basically, that news feels like a million birthday presents

being handed to me at once. Heni believes me! Now all I

need to do is reverse this curse. I look around the room,

panic racing through me. There are students in the class-

room, watching Big Poppy talking to her cat. I fear the

weirder she looks, the lower my reputation plummets.

"Hide me in my desk," I say. "When it's time to go out-

side during the eclipse, grab the art, then I'll jump in your

solar eclipse box."

"Kids have already seen you," Big Poppy whispers to me.

"Heni, of course, but also Max, Theo, and Rowan."

I look around. Reality hurts. Max, Theo, and Rowan are

on the science rug staring at us. They look stunned.

Big Poppy clears her throat. "So . . . I'm having a tiny

problem. And I need to hide my cat in my desk for the

morning. I'd prefer you guys didn't tell anybody, especially Ms. Gish. Cool?"

Any second the warning bell will ring and the room will fill.

"Poppy wouldn't ask us to do this if it wasn't super important," Heni gushes.

"Okay," Max says. "I like cats."

"Is it your emotional support animal?" Theo asks. "My grandma has one of those to help with her hearing problems. It's a ferret."

"If Ms. Gish asks me directly if you have a cat in your desk, I'm not going to lie," Rowan says.

"Fair," Big Poppy says. "You are all very awesome people. Thank you!"

Ring!

The warning bell goes off and Big Poppy screams. What?! Why did she do that? No one even looks at her. What world is this?

Getting stuffed inside my own desk before anybody else sees me feels very exciting. I cozy up to my old pencil case, and art spiral, and math notebook. It smells like pencil shavings and metal and hope in here. Hearing the hubbub of my class makes my stomach flip. I didn't realize how much I missed everybody. When I move my head to the desk's corner I can see a tiny sliver of the floor. Oh my stars! I recognize those pink shimmery Mary Jane shoes.

"Good afternoon, Kit," Big Poppy says, sounding very tense. "What do you need?"

"I'm letting you know that I spoke to Ms. Dance this morning. And she's letting me try out to be a pony again."

"Wow," Big Poppy says. "That's nuts."

"It's not nuts!" Kit says. "It's understandable. I have a doctor's note explaining that I had a rash that day." *Sniff. Sniff.* "Anyway, why does your desk smell like fish?"

"It doesn't," Big Poppy says.

"It does," Kit says. "Super stinky fish."

"Well, why do your shoes smell like sad mushrooms?" Big Poppy says. "Odors are everywhere."

"You are so weird and rude," Kit says. "I can't believe we were ever friends."

"I know," Big Poppy says. "It's shocking."

I sit very still as I listen to Big Poppy talk to Kit. None of these are things I would say, but I can't help admiring her for being so fierce and honest. After we switch back, I need to be more like that. I can't keep being a scaredy-cat. No more bossy friends. Just good friends. Which means I'll need to be making a few new ones.

"All right, class," Ms. Gish says. "We've got a busy morning. After I take roll we all need to grab our solar eclipse boxes and head outside. We've got our first play practice after that."

I hold my breath. Everything is about to happen.

Then, out of nowhere, dusky-rose ballerina flats approach Big Poppy's desk.

"I'm so proud of you, Poppy," Ms. Gish says. "You're the only fifth grader who even tried out for a lead part."

"Thanks," Big Poppy exclaims.

Ugh. Why does my cat have to be so interested in live theater? What a nightmare. If I actually do get my life back, I'm going to have to adjust to a million big changes.

When everyone stands up to go, Heni waits beside my desk along with Max and Theo, who make a curtain with their bodies, so when Big Poppy lifts me out, nobody sees me climb into her solar eclipse box. There's one pinprick of light streaming into this dark square. I take small breaths and curl myself into a ball.

This is it. In the next few minutes I'll learn whether or not I get my life back. Excitement and fear pulse through me. Either it will happen or it won't. This is the most pressure I've ever felt.

I hear the sound of paper being pulled down from the bulletin board. "Uh-oh," Big Poppy says.

"Why is your art project falling apart?" Heni asks.

"I might have spilled some milk on it," Big Poppy says. "And tried to dry it out in the sun. And then left it in my backpack for a few days. Can you help me? Grab as many pieces as you can."

"Make sure to get *all* the pieces!" I meow-shout. We'll need the *entire* art project to make this work.

"Is this a piece?" Heni asks.

"That's just some garbage," Theo says.

"What about this one?" Heni asks again.

"I think that's a crushed cracker," Max explains.

Crunch. "You're right," Big Poppy says, making what are clearly chewing sounds. "I keep a short stack in my desk."

Did Big Poppy just eat a stepped-on floor cracker? How can she possibly have an appetite at a time like this? How is it even possible that pieces of trash and the most important art project I ever made are indistinguishable? Augh! My entire future rides on what happens next. Am I the only cat in this room who understands this?

CHAPTER 23

In the Weeds

Old Poppy slides around inside the box as I carry her to the grass field beside the school. Heni walks so close to me that I can hear her boots smoosh across the damp ground right behind me. It's exciting to focus on Old Poppy and our big switch-back and listen to Heni talk. What could be more perfect than Old Poppy, the real Poppy, getting her life back beside her chatty best friend, who apparently has successfully reached a new allergy-free status?

"After this is all over, I'm thinking maybe I should sit on your bed and see if I can tolerate Mitten Man's—I mean Poppy's—I mean Mitten Man's dander," Heni says. "We can time it, and I can see if I'm really better."

"Sure," I say.

"Maybe this week," Heni says.

"Cool," I say.

"Maybe tomorrow," Heni says.

"If all your allergies really are fixed, how would you feel about getting your own cat?" I ask. "I know one that needs a home."

"I'd love that!" Heni says.

"I'll keep my fingers and my toes crossed," I say.

"Poppy, I've missed you so much!" Heni gushes. She aims that comment at the box, but it also feels like she's talking to me. Her words feel so pure. Heni Kanoa truly has missed Poppy McBean. And what comes out of my mouth next, even though her shoulder keeps bumping mine, isn't even a lie. "I've really missed you too," I say. I don't feel so mad anymore that she left Old Poppy splattered on the hallway. She apologized, which is a skill I now know most humans don't have. And no one can stay stuck on a puke bucket forever. "You're such a normal, kind, good person." And I'm not saying that for Old Poppy's sake. I'm saying it because it feels true.

"Poppy, that's so sweet!" If I wasn't holding a cat in a box, I know Heni would clobber me with hugs. But she understands that I'm carrying precious cargo, so she doesn't, flashing me a smile so bright it would outshine a thousand rainbows.

"I think it's go time," I say, trying to transition us out of friendship gush and into action mode. "Let's get as far away from teachers as possible."

"Won't the sidewalk be a good escape path home for Mitten Man?" Heni asks, and we gravitate into the gravelly gutter.

"Please stay on the grass," Principal Savage says loudly into a handheld blowhorn, throwing some stink eye our way.

I nod. She's right. After we switch back, if it happens, I'll be able to use this route to get to the street and can follow the road back home. I figure once everybody is paying attention to the eclipse, I can whip Old Poppy out of the box and plop her on the art project pieces, we can say our wishes, and voilà, magic will finally happen again.

Principal Savage blasts more information in our faces. "Whatever you do, don't look directly at the sun. And don't think sunglasses will help. You need lenses that follow safety recommendations from NASA to fully protect yourself from solar radiation. That's why we made these boxes, re-member."

"This almost feels too dangerous," Heni says.

I'm reminded of the time I faced down an eagle in an open field. Or woke up in a garter snake den. Or when I outran a rock chuck and hid in an earth berm root cellar. Everything right now feels *more* dangerous than any of that.

"Now, everybody, put your boxes on your heads," Principal Savage says.

Oh no. That's the one thing I can't do. But I also can't tell her that. What are my options?

I can see Ms. Gish parting a path through some sixth graders. She's headed toward me. I can't risk staying here and letting somebody take Old Poppy or my art project away from me.

I need to do something.

"Heni," I say. "I'm gonna try to run home."

"What?" she asks. "That's a mile away!"

"We're all about to have our minds blown," Principal Savage says. "Get ready for the temperature dip. Bright stars and planets will soon be visible too."

Ms. Gish is so close to me, I can smell her sweet perfume.

"Boxes up!" Principal Savage commands.

I reach inside my box, pull out Old Poppy, and clutch her to my chest. I need to give her back her life. It's time.

"Were we allowed to bring a pet to this?" a girl asks.

"Poppy McBean has a cat!" Kit shouts.

And I'm off.

It's actually difficult to run top speed while carrying a cat, a disintegrating art project, and a solar eclipse box, so I drop the box.

"Poppy!" Ms. Gish yells. "Come back! It's a serious offense to leave school grounds!"

The sky begins to darken. It doesn't feel like night. But this darkness hovers over me in a peculiar way.

"What we're experiencing now is called a path of totality," Principal Savage booms. But his voice gets smaller the farther I run.

"Where are you going?" Ms. Gish calls.

"Home!" I reply.

I don't want anybody to worry about me.

"Meow! Meow! Meow!"

"Don't yell at me," I say. "I know this isn't a perfect solution. Would I prefer you seamlessly switch back at school undetected? Yes! But I really didn't see an option for that." Old Poppy needs to trust me. Because when the two of us work together, we really, truly, honestly make a good team.

The longer I run, the warmer I feel, even as the dark shadow lifts, bringing everything around me back into light. Did we miss it? Is the eclipse over? Am I still a girl? "Make your wish!" I yell at Old Poppy. For a moment, I think maybe I need to get all the way back to the garage for the magic to happen, in which case, I'm out of luck, because I'm so exhausted I need to walk now, and I know somebody is still chasing me. I set Old Poppy down in the grass and try to piece the art project back together.

"Hurry! Hurry!" I say. "This needs to be the fastest puzzle we ever put together!"

But isn't a *real* solar eclipse better than a cheap paper copy of an eclipse? I've got to believe that the sun and moon are bringing their own magic and big energy to this moment. And maybe Aunt Blanche was right about something.

I think back to what she said about my collar: *Crystals turn especially powerful when certain times are upon us, like the upcoming eclipse.*

"It's happening!" I say in an urgent voice. "We've got the real thing. Sit next to me and make your wish!"

As Old Poppy hurries to sit beside me, a bright spray of sunshine drenches us both. It's time for me to make my wish. I say those five simple words I thought before in the garage during the first swap: "I wish Poppy felt happy." Immediately, I feel something I've only felt one time before. The switch.

Last time when the switch happened, it felt sharp and intense, like I was being yanked into spaghetti noodles, my arms and legs pulled longer and longer as a bright buzz hummed through my bones. This time, it's much more mellow. The sensation of being gently squished feels so tender and comforting, like I've become Jell-O, and I tumble into a clump of wild raspberry bushes. Is this right? All of my fingers feel loose and fuzzy, and every last piece of myself grows foggy and calm. I close my eyes. Bright lights swirl wildly on the inside of my eyelids.

Then I smell a bitter dust so strong my eyes flip back open. Scotch broom! The grass around me has burst up dramatically, turning my world into a prickly forest. I try to sit up, but feel something whip behind me. My wonderful fluffy tail! It happened. I am me. Poppy is Poppy. I'm normal again. Which means I never have to spend another miserable day in a classroom surrounded by fifth graders. I get to poop in a box again. And somebody else has to scoop it!

Before either of us have time to say anything, I hear the sound of giant footsteps in the grass. Holy donkey butts. Ms. Gish is in the Scotch broom with us. I turn to Poppy and tell her.

"You go back to school," I say. "I'll run home."

But her face just looks sad and panicked. "I can't understand you," she whispers. "All I hear are meows. Go home. I'll fix things with my teacher."

At first I don't move. Poppy can't understand me? How is that possible?

"Wait!" she says, jerking me back into her arms. I feel her unthread the collar from my neck. "This is too dangerous for you to wear." Poppy pockets it. "Now go!" she screams. "Before you get captured."

I take off and race for home. Running on four quick feet, I feel so free. I zoom through thick weeds faster than ever. Wind in my ears. Breeze in my fur. I bet Poppy will be able to understand me when she gets home. I bet the trauma of being captured by your teacher in a raspberry bush after leaving school grounds during a solar eclipse stunned her brain and it just needs some time to recover. Things are about to return to the way they were, or even better, an upgraded life for me and for Poppy. Take that, world!

CHAPTER 24
Cat Status

Meow. Meow. Meow. Meow. Meow. Meow. Meow. Meow.
Meow. Meow. Meow. Meow. Meow. Meow. Meow. Meow.
Meow. Meow. Meow. Meow. Meow. Meow. Meow. Meow.
Meow. Meow. Meow. Meow. Meow. Meow. Meow. Meow.
Meow. Meow. Meow. Meow. Meow. Meow. Meow. Meow.
Meow. Meow. Meow. Meow. Meow. Meow. Meow. Meow.
Meow. Meow. Meow. Meow. Meow. Meow. Meow. Meow.
Meow. Meow. Meow. Meow. Meow. Meow. Meow. Meow.
Meow. Meow. Meow. Meow. Meow. Meow. Meow. Meow.
Meow. Meow. Meow. Meow. Meow. Meow. Meow. Meow.
Meow. Meow. Meow. Meow. Meow. Meow. Meow. Meow.
Meow. Meow. Meow. Meow. Meow. Meow. Meow. Meow.
Meow. Meow. Meow. Meow. Meow. Meow. Meow. Meow.
Meow. Meow. Meow. Meow. Meow. Meow. Meow. Meow.
Meow. Meow. Meow. Meow. Meow. Meow. Meow. Meow.

Meow. Meow. Meow. Meow. Meow. Meow. Meow. Meow.
Meow. Meow. Meow. Meow. Meow. Meow. Meow. Meow.
Meow. Meow. Meow. Meow. Meow. Meow. Meow. Meow.
Meow. Meow. Meow. Meow. Meow. Meow. Meow. Meow.
Meow. Meow. Meow. Meow. Meow. Meow. Meow. Meow.
Meow. Meow. Meow. Meow. Meow. Meow. Meow. Meow.
Meow. Meow. Meow. Meow. Meow. Meow. Meow. Meow.
Meow. Meow. Meow. Meow. Meow. Meow. Meow. Meow.
Meow. Meow. Meow. Meow. Meow. Meow. Meow. Meow.
Meow. Meow. Meow. Meow. Meow. Meow. Meow.

CHAPTER 25

Dirty Thief

Had anybody told me at the start of fifth grade that I'd leave school property during a solar eclipse with my cat and a semi-stolen art project and receive absolutely zero punishment, I wouldn't have believed it. But that's exactly what's happening. Because Mom didn't enter the principal's office acting like a mom. She entered this room acting like a detective.

"Principal Savage, the only way Mitten Man could've escaped is if an intruder broke into our house and let him out," Mom says. "There *have* been robberies in the neighborhood. We need to call the police!"

And when your mom calls the police while you're in the principal's office, the energy in the room really shifts. So instead of punishing me, everything turned into a plan to get home and document the break-in.

"Grab your things and let's go, Poppy," Mom barks. "The police are on their way."

"I hope this all gets sorted out," Principal Savage calls after us.

We're almost to the car before I feel brave enough to offer a counter story to the break-in theory. "Maybe Mitten Man broke out on his own," I offer. "He's very smart."

"Poppy, it's better to accept that we have criminals in our neighborhood than to fictionalize this situation and give your cat superpowers," she says.

And when Mom uses a giant word like *fictionalize*, it means she's thinking super hard about her own idea and isn't really interested in entertaining others. It's a huge bummer. There's so much I want to tell her but can't. She should know that Aunt Blanche doubled back to do the right thing. It seems important. But how would I know what Aunt Blanche did if I was at school? And what's the point of trying to convince Mom that Mitten Man did actually open the window himself? She won't believe it.

And here's the other thing. Deezil and Whip *have* been stealing items out of our garage for weeks. I mean, isn't stealing a turtle a real crime? Couldn't somebody face jail time or at least a hefty fine over it? They should. So I let what's happening continue to happen.

Mom takes pictures of the open kitchen window while I stand near her on the patio. Dad's on the scene too.

"So here's where the thief gained entry," she says. "We need to triple-check that nothing is missing. I'll go through my jewelry again. Don, you should go through your tools."

"Dad's in the garage going through his tools," I say. "He can't hear you."

Turns out Mom documents a crime scene with exceptional precision.

"Whatever they used to cut the screen doesn't look like a knife."

I lean forward and see the jagged tears where Death Tiger clawed out the screen.

"I think my best guess is that Mitten Man made his exit out the kitchen window and startled the thief, making him or her take off before he or she actually stole anything," Mom says.

"Wrong!" Dad says, exiting the garage with a notebook. "The thief took a bunch of stuff from the garage."

"Drat!" Mom says. "Your power tools?"

"Oddly, no," he says. "They took an old wrench, a damaged coffee mug where I kept old screws, a can of violet spray paint, a package of tortillas from the deep freezer, and a small plastic pickle."

"Are you sure?" I ask. Because that sounds an awful lot like the items that Whip placed on top of Raul. I can't believe they stole all that stuff from our garage. "Is any of our pancake mix missing?" I ask, but Dad's on a roll.

"I'm a million percent sure," Dad says. "The garage might not look orderly to you, but I've got my own method for keeping track of things."

"Where did you keep the pickle?" Mom asks.

"On the tool table next to the flower pot," he says. "It squeaked when you squoze it. I was saving it for the propane Christmas party for my white elephant gift."

"Huh," Mom says. "I feel like this break-in has shed new light on our garage and its vulnerabilities. So speaking of shedding light, we need motion-sensor lights. Multiple ones. Stat."

It's amazing to think that if my parents had thought of security lights a month ago, our lives would have turned out so different. No Deezil. No Whip. Probably no Raul or Death Tiger either. Where would I have ended up without Death Tiger?

"I agree," Dad says. "Plus, I just scared a bat out of the garage. So we should probably add some lights inside too."

"Good idea," I say. After having lived outdoors and spent time in the dark garage, adding lights makes a ton of sense. A well-lit area is always a safer place to be.

"What kind of bat?" my mom asks.

My dad puts on his serious face. "It was brown and fierce. I had to use two brooms to scoot it out."

"Maybe the *bat* scared the thief away," my mom muses.

"I can't believe the police haven't come yet," Dad says.

"They will," Mom says. "They've got some other break-ins they're investigating. I bet it's one dirty thief robbing this whole area."

"Or two in cahoots," I say, then realize I'm giving away more than I should know. "I'm gonna go and hang out with Mitten Man."

"That's a great idea," Mom says.

"We'll keep checking out the garage," Dad says.

And that's why my first time in the house as a person again, I'm all alone. It feels magical and perfect, like the time my parents rented a pony for my birthday and all my friends sang "Happy Birthday" to me while I sat on top of it and my dad carried over a four-layer unicorn cake with a turquoise mane. Even the air in the kitchen smells marvelous. I use my hands to open the refrigerator and turn on and off the water! I pour a glass of lemonade! I head to the bathroom and flush the toilet!

Just then Mitten Man trots around the corner and gives me a yawn.

Meow. Meow. Meow.

A twinge of regret teeters through me. I keep my eyes locked on his, but my ability to understand the language of meow seems to be gone. I reach down and pick up my cat and cradle his warm furry body in my arms.

"I can't understand you anymore," I say.

I look in his eyes. I want to believe he still knows what I'm saying, even though I can't decipher one meow from the next. "I want to believe you can still understand me," I tell him. "Can you?"

314

Sometimes Mitten Man resists being held close, but right now he lets it happen. He snuggles against me and I kiss the top of his head.

"I've got news," I say. "Death Tiger will go to Heni like you planned, so all the animals will have good homes! Yay!" I should probably mention to the eighth graders how much good I'm really doing for animals.

Then I remember the collar in my pocket. I slide Mitten Man onto my pillow and pull it out.

"You can't wear this anymore. It needs to stay in a place where nobody can ever find it. Dad already ordered you another one, anyway."

I know the perfect hiding spot. I crawl on my hands and knees to the very back of my closet. The back corner carpet lifts up, and I place the collar underneath it. Then I press it back down and put my snow boots over it. Nobody will ever find it. Everything feels safe.

Except I don't see Mitten Man back on my bed. Where could he have gone? Panic leaps through me. But my bedroom door is shut, and it's not like he's a wizard. He's still in the room somewhere. I hear a scratching sound underneath my bed. I roll onto the floor and lift up my lacy bed skirt.

"What are you doing?" I ask.

He's scratching a spiral notebook with a red checker on it. Mitten Man sits on top of it as I drag them both to me.

CAN YOU UNDERSTAND ME? It's in my handwriting, but I don't remember writing it.

It takes me a second to realize that this is something Mitten Man must have written back when he was Big Poppy. He's written the words *YES* and *NO* at the bottom of the page. I set the checker down in the middle, between the two words. Mitten Man gently places one white paw on the checker. He slides it slowly to the word *NO*.

Wait. But if he could understand me, wouldn't he have slid the checker to *YES*?

His tiny pink mouth cracks open, and he looks at me. I think I see him almost smile. Then he slides the checker to *YES* and sets his paw on the carpet next to my knee.

"Are you being serious?" I ask. Tears pool behind my eyes.

Mitten Man taps the red checker again. I scoop him up in my arms and try not to get tears on him; he hates water. This is the most amazing thing that has ever happened to me. What is Heni going to think when I tell her? The news makes my whole life seem even more wonderful than it did two minutes ago. I gently rub his head. "This is all so crazy," I tell him. "We switch places and you mix up my friendships and eat lunch with eighth graders and make me a clown. And I get all your animal friends safely back to where they belong. But it doesn't even matter because everything worked out. I mean, don't be too proud of yourself. You caused a ton of drama. And I risked my life multiple times. But I'm going to be okay. You're going to be okay. We're all going to be okay."

Six Weeks Later

Everybody around me rushes to get ready for our first dress rehearsal. Costume pieces fly from one set of hands to another. Shimmer shoes. Furry vests. Dog collars. Streamer tails. The excitement makes me feel buzzy and nervous. Sadly, Ms. Dance piled on clown makeup so thick my face feels like it's coated in plastic. My cheeks no longer feel like my cheeks. Neither do my eyelids. Or my nostrils.

"You look super amazing," Heni says, holding up a small round mirror for me to see my bright red, white, and yellow face.

"I'm nervous about using the microphone," I say.

"I'm nervous about our pony-swish sequence. During practice, both my shoes fell off," Heni says, flashing me a freaked-out smile.

That would be terrible. No matter what happens to me, I know I'm not going to lose my shoes.

"I need to check in with my herd," Heni says.

I watch her gallop off to be with the other ponies. I do wish I could've practiced with Heni and Rosario after all. Once they learned the routine, they weren't stressed out at all about the choreography. And seeing Kit get reassigned from dog pack to pony squad taught me an important life lesson. If you've got a doctor's note and complain enough, you can get almost any decision reversed.

"You look so cool, Poppy," says one of the dogs.

It's hard to recognize everybody in their costumes. This dog is made up to look like a King Charles spaniel. Gold crown on his head. Soft, floppy ears. Brown and white face.

"You look cool too," I say.

He barks at me and hurries off.

"Wow!" Heni says, rushing up to me. "I can't believe you paid Deezil Wolfinger a compliment."

"That was Deezil?" I ask. He's moving in a super fluid and happy way, not like his regular bully stomping manner. He must really like theater.

"He's actually amazing," Rosario says.

Heni, Rosario, and I crowd together at the side of the stage to watch the dogs rehearse. I'd been so focused on my

319

own role that I hadn't paid much attention to the group numbers. Deezil does seem to have much more pizazz than I'd expect. He holds the light of the stage brighter than any of the other dogs. And his voice seems louder too.

"My only wish is for a full dog dish. How I love being a dog!"

After the dogs burst into song they do a series of kicks, followed by intense air digging. Deezil outshines everybody.

"So weird that he used to be really bad," Heni says. "And then like magic he turned great."

"And that it happened overnight," Rosario adds.

"The clown goes on next," Ms. Dance says, marking my name off her clipboard.

"All I want! My biggest wish! Let me be a dog! Bark! Bark! Bark!"

It's silly for me to think that Deezil is anybody other than Deezil, even if he's acting completely differently.

Just to be safe, I'll check on the collar when I get home. I mean, I'm sure I'm overreacting. Being turned into a cat probably will have lingering effects on my trust levels for months.

"Poppy! Go!" Ms. Dance commands.

I walk to the center of the stage in my floppy shoes. I don't have to dance too much. I don't have to sing. I don't have to act like a super-crazy clown. I just have to deliver my lines. Mitten Man secured this role for me, and I want to do the best I can.

"I'm trotting along when suddenly,

every piece of me feels all rubbery.

You laugh your heads off when I trip and fall down,

sure nothing can hurt me because I'm a clown.

Not true. Look, I've got an actual heart.

When I play this big klutz, it's just a part.

Like weirdos and oddballs who will not conform,

our feelings are REAL. Got it? Let the ponies perform!"

As I'm leaving the stage I don't want to walk off in a boring way. An idea comes to me. What a perfect time to show everybody my power dance move. *Double kick! Cross stomp! Swisher arms! Shuffle jump! Ta-da!* Everyone erupts in applause and the curtains close. From my head to my toes, I feel happy and lucky, and totally like myself.

NOTE TO READER:

I bet this story shocked the socks right off of you. I know it's hard to believe that such wild magic exists in this world. I'm living proof that it does. Probably, I'm telling this story more for myself than for you. Now that I'm old, when I look back on everything, the ups, the downs, my friends, my frenemies, my mind spends the most time thinking about my loyal owner and all the fun times we had together. So maybe my mother was right after all. Remember? "Baby, you were born under a lucky star. You'll spend your whole life brightening the lives of others." Of course, Poppy brightened my life too. As did a few other people. That's what living is all about. All I know is that nobody will ever compare to Poppy McBean. Seriously. Where would I be—*who would I be*—without her?

ACKNOWLEDGMENTS:

Let me begin by saying that without my cat, Bunny, this book would not exist. He was such a good boy and traveled along with me on all my adventures, from Kalamazoo to San Francisco to Rhode Island to Los Angeles. Had we ever swapped places, I have no doubt that he would have swiftly ruined my life. A true cat through and through, he dwells everywhere inside this book. Thank you, Bunny. And where would I be without Sara Crowe, who has been my agent for almost twenty years and has managed to sell the many, many books I've sent her? This one took many years for me to get right, and she never nudged me about it. She's perfect that way. Also, I feel very, very, very lucky to have encountered the brain of editor extraordinaire Taylor Norman, who read and reread and provided critical notes that turned this manuscript into the book of my dreams. I'm beyond grateful to her. I eagerly open every email she sends me, and when we have phone calls, I'm always bummed when they end. She's that good. I'm also incredibly grateful to the entire team at Chronicle Books and beyond. Especially to the copy editor, Mikayla Butchart; proofreaders, Margo Winton Parodi and Judith Riotto; and managing editorial team, Claire Fletcher and Lucy Medrich, who were all very good at catching all the things. And to the design and production crew, Jay Marvel and Kevin Armstrong, who made a thousand decisions that made this book beautiful. And to Celia Krampien, for the gorgeous cover. And to Carrie Gao, Mikaela Luke, Caitlin Ek, Andie Krawczyk, Mary Duke, and the rest of the marketing and sales team. I'm also very grateful to my bonus editor, Elizabeth Lazowski, who helped the book get to the finish line and kindly told me to take the whole weekend to write these acknowledgments, which allowed me to sleep like a normal person and not stress out about forgetting all the important people. Furthermore, I'm lucky to be married to a writer, and I am eternally grateful to my husband, Brian Evenson, who read this story as I slowly built it and always told me the parts he thought were funny. I'm equally lucky to be the mother of a voracious reader, Max, and I'm thankful that he also likes to read my work while it's still fresh and messy and that he always offers encouragement and radical suggestions. My family is the best, and I'm happy that I feel that way even when I'm not writing my acknowledgments. I'm grateful for my friend Claudia Rankine, who invited me on a retreat to work on this book when I was just getting it off the ground, even though the retreat mostly turned into a museum hop and shopping trip in New York. I started it there, and sometimes starting can be the hardest part. I also want to thank my pet sitters Jackie, Nancy, Bill, Bengte, Paras, Theo, and my dad, who at various times watched Bunny and in some cases even let him live with them. You made our lives better, and I'll always be grateful. I'd also like to thank my friend Joy Harjo for letting me use a line from one of her poems for the epigraph. Her work is something I turn to always. There are many unnamed friends and family who helped make this book real and alive, and I want you to know that I'm thankful for you too. I'm lucky to have you all in my life. Especially my sister Julie.

Lastly, I want to thank my mother, Patti Tracy, who, for the last three years, talked to me many times a week, even on her chemo days, while I wrote and edited this book. She was the first writer in the family, sometimes using the name River Ames. I will miss our conversations.